The Case of the Reliable Russian Spaniels

A Thousand Islands Doggy Inn Mystery

B.R. Snow

This book is a work of fiction. Names, characters, places and events are either used fictitiously or are the product of the author's imagination. All rights reserved, including the right to reproduce this book, or portions thereof, in any form. No part of this text may be reproduced, transmitted, downloaded, decompiled, or stored in or introduced into any information storage and retrieval system, in any form by any means, whether electronic or mechanical without the express written consent of the author. The scanning, uploading, and distribution of this book via the Internet or any other means without the permission of the publisher are illegal and punishable by law.

Copyright © 2018 B.R. Snow

ISBN: 978-1-942691-50-1

Website: www.brsnow.net/

Twitter: @BernSnow

Facebook: facebook.com/bernsnow

Cover Design: Reggie Cullen

Cover Photo: James R. Miller

Other Books by B.R. Snow

The Thousand Islands Doggy Inn Mysteries

- The Case of the Abandoned Aussie
- The Case of the Brokenhearted Bulldog
- The Case of the Caged Cockers
- The Case of the Dapper Dandie Dinmont
- The Case of the Eccentric Elkhound
- The Case of the Faithful Frenchie
- The Case of the Graceful Goldens
- The Case of the Hurricane Hounds
- The Case of the Itinerant Ibizan
- The Case of the Jaded Jack Russell
- The Case of the Klutz King Charles
- The Case of the Lovable Labs
- The Case of the Mellow Maltese
- The Case of the Natty Newfie
- The Case of the Overdue Otterhound
- The Case of the Prescient Poodle
- The Case of the Quizzical Queens Beagle

The Whiskey Run Chronicles

- Episode 1 – The Dry Season Approaches
- Episode 2 – Friends and Enemies
- Episode 3 – Let the Games Begin
- Episode 4 – Enter the Revenuer
- Episode 5 – A Changing Landscape
- Episode 6 – Entrepreneurial Spirits
- Episode 7 – All Hands On Deck
- The Whiskey Run Chronicles – The Complete Volume 1
- The Whiskey Run Chronicles – The Complete Volume 2

The Damaged Posse

- American Midnight
- Larrikin Gene
- Sneaker World
- Summerman
- The Duplicates

Other Novels

- Divorce Hotel
- Either Ore

To Michele

Friends like you are hard to find

Chapter 1

Sunday

Despite producing the urge to scratch the freezer burn covering most of the right side of my face, the overhead misting system inside the cabana felt great and provided a welcome respite from the temperature that was already over a hundred and climbing. I lightly ran my fingernails over the patch of dry skin and glanced around the tented area littered with a variety of poolside survival items. Damp, grease-stained magazines were scattered on the tile along with a couple of paperback mysteries I hadn't had a chance to pick up, much less read. Numerous towels, both damp and dry, mingled with tubes of sunscreen, and a large bottle of Ibuprofen on one of the lounge chairs was partially buried beneath an impressive collection of empty water bottles. A half-drunk Mimosa sat by itself on a small table near the outside edge of the spacious cabana.

I still hadn't figured out who'd had the courage to order a cocktail after last night, but I had to applaud their commitment.

Quite a crew, I said to myself as I replayed the previous evening's highlights then took another look around the cabana.

Millie had her arms draped over two gorgeous Russian spaniels and was chatting quietly with Jill, who was nursing a massive hangover and making no attempt to hide it. Which was a smart decision on her part: It would have been easier to hide an elephant under her lounge chair. Jill had inexplicably challenged my mother to a drinking contest last night while we were watching a dance troupe of male strippers. She'd been no match for my mother.

One of the spaniels was still holding the stick she'd discovered during a recent walk and wasn't about to give it up. The other dog rolled over onto his back and stretched. His legs stuck straight up in the air, and his tongue lolled as the mist wafted over him. I reached out and patted the spaniel's stomach, and he thumped his tail softly against the thick, soft cushion.

If the spaniel could have talked, I was pretty sure he'd be saying…*aah*.

Josie and Chef Claire got up and made the short walk to the edge of the massive swimming pool. Josie, much the worse for wear, was taking baby steps and moving at a snail's pace.

"Be careful your stitches don't get wet," I said.

"At the moment, I couldn't care if they fell out," Josie said, glancing at the enormous bandage covering her wrist and forearm. "Actually, right now, I couldn't care if my arm fell *off*."

"Hungover?" I said, laughing.

"What do you think?" she said, making a face at me.

"Try the hair of the dog. That might make you feel better."

"Today would be more like hair of the kennel." Then she turned to Chef Claire. "We should probably stay in the shallow end. I'm not sure I'm going to be able to move my arms and legs."

2

Chef Claire managed a small nod, then dove in. Josie followed suit, and I watched them swim away then stand up in waist-high water. They both rubbed their temples in an impromptu synchronized swimming move, and I felt my own mild hangover return. I looked over at my mother who was removing chips of various colors from her purse and counting them.

"How are you feeling, Mom?"

"I feel wonderful, darling," she said, grimacing as she gingerly shifted in her chair. "Thanks for asking."

"How is that possible?" I said, staring at her in disbelief. "I've never seen you drink that much before."

"That's because you're never invited to the really good parties."

"Funny, Mom," I said. "What on earth were you thinking having a drinking contest with Jill?"

"It was her idea," she said, shrugging. "And I couldn't back down from the challenge. Besides, isn't that the sort of thing we're supposed to do at a pre-wedding girls' getaway?"

"I suppose," I said. "How many shots of tequila did you have?"

"Well, let's see," she said, building a large stack of purple chips I knew were worth five grand each. "I believe it was eight. No, nine. I forgot about the one I drank out of that dancer's navel."

"Yeah, who could forget that?" I said, laughing as I reached for my phone. "Fortunately, we don't have to worry about it. I've got it memorialized."

3

"Let me see that thing," she said, snatching the phone out of my hand and promptly deleting all the photos. She handed the phone back and shrugged. "He was cute."

"I already emailed them home."

"Why am I not surprised?" she said, reaching out to examine my freezer burn. "Does it still hurt?"

"Only when people touch it," I said, swatting her hand away. "Do you think it'll be gone before the wedding?"

"If it isn't, we'll just shoot all the photos in profile."

"Yeah, good one, Mom. How's your butt?" I said with a grin.

"It's fine," she said, obviously not wanting to discuss it.

"Note to self," I said, laughing. "Never do cannonballs into a hot tub."

"I slipped," she said, giving me the evil eye. "But it was a good after-party."

"I'll take your word for it."

Chef Claire climbed out of the pool then extended a hand to Josie who grabbed it and eventually managed to get out of the water. They slowly made their way back to the cabana and stretched out on their loungers.

"Feel better?" I said.

"It's gonna take a lot more than a dip in the pool to make that happen," Josie said, putting her sunglasses on. "I need food."

"How's your arm, dear?" my mother said.

"Probably about the same as your butt, Mrs. C.," Josie said.

"Are you sure Bugsy is going to be okay?" my mother said.

"Yeah, he's fine," Josie said.

"I've never seen anything like him before," Chef Claire said. "How big did Hedaya say he is?"

"Thirteen feet," Josie said.

"That's incredible," Chef Claire said. "I had no idea a lizard could get that big."

"Or scratch like that," I said, shaking my head at the memory.

"The little bugger," Josie said. "I should have let him choke to death."

"Well, I'm glad you didn't," my mother said, getting up from her chair. "Hedaya was so grateful, he's comping us."

"Where are you going?" I said.

"To go win some more money, where else?" my mother said, sliding the chips back into her purse. "I'll be back in a couple of hours."

She waved and did her best to walk without limping as she made her way around the pool and into the casino.

"How does she do it?" I said, staring after her.

"I think it's called having a zest for life," Chef Claire said.

"You guys want to order some food?" Josie said, glancing over at Millie and Jill.

"Sounds great," Millie said.

"Yeah, I have to eat something," Jill said, slowly nodding her head. "I need to take some more aspirin and don't want to do it on an empty stomach."

"Good call," Chef Claire said, laughing. "Based on what we heard last night, I'm pretty sure your stomach is empty."

"I think it was a mistake to try pole dancing at the club," Jill said. "You know, that's probably what got my stomach gurgling."

"Yeah, I'm sure that was it," Chef Claire said, still laughing.

"Uh, I hate to tell you, Jill," Millie said, shaking her head at the memory. "That wasn't actually a pole you were on."

"It wasn't?"

"No, that was a street sign," Millie said. "At the corner of Tropicana and Las Vegas Boulevard."

"Really?" she said, surprised by that bit of news. Then she grimaced as if it hurt to even think about last night. "Well, that explains the bus tokens mixed in with the dollar bills I found in my shorts this morning," Jill said.

"What a trip," Chef Claire said.

"Memorable," Josie said, grimacing. "Promise me this is the only time you'll get married."

"I'll see what I can do," I said, glancing around. "Yeah, it's almost been perfect."

"You mean, apart from the dead Russians, right?" Josie said, raising an eyebrow.

"Yeah, apart from that," I said, glancing at the spaniels who were softly snoring in the mist.

I replayed the last few days in my head and decided, on balance, it still could be accurately described as a good trip.

Two dead Russians.

6

A thirteen-foot Komodo dragon.

One gold key.

Thirty-seven stitches.

An incredible hot streak at the craps table.

My mother, the winner of an ill-advised drinking contest, cannonballing into a hot tub.

Jill suspended upside down on a street sign that had attracted the attention of dozens of onlookers, including a couple of local cops who hadn't appreciated the show.

A freezer burn on the side of my face that was threatening to leave me with a permanent reminder of our trip spent in air-conditioned comfort interspersed with daily lounge sessions by the pool in the scorching sun of a Vegas July.

And two gorgeous Russian spaniels who'd be making the trip home with us to take up permanent residence in Clay Bay.

It's been a bizarre series of events that probably could have only happened in Vegas. And while I know that what happens here is supposed to stay here, I'm sure this is a story we'll be retelling for years to come.

Confused?

Join the club.

But I'm getting ahead of myself, so let's back up a bit.

Chapter 2

Wednesday

I made the short walk from the limo to the casino entrance without breaking a sweat then stepped inside the chill and looked around at the stylish Oriental décor. I draped an arm around my mother's shoulders and pulled her in close for a hug.

"This is nice, Mom," I said, continuing to take in the surroundings. "Good call."

"Yes, Hedaya does a wonderful job," she said, heading for the registration area.

"How do you know this guy?"

"He used to have a place on Grand Cayman," she said, coming to a stop in front of a smiling clerk. "Good morning."

"Welcome to Hedaya," the woman said, glancing around at our group of six. "Could I have your last name, please?"

"Chandler," my mother said. "We have a reservation for two adjoining suites."

"Yes, I see that right here," she said, tapping her keyboard then beaming at my mother. "Mr. Hedaya asked to be informed as soon as you arrived. Please, bear with me for a moment." She made a short phone call then hung up and accepted the credit card my mother was holding out. "He'll be right out."

"He's such a sweet man," my mother said, glancing around while we waited.

8

Moments later, an elderly Chinese man who was ninety if he was a day approached and beamed at my mother and extended his hand. Then they shared a warm embrace.

"It's so good to see you," he said, completing the greeting with a small bow before taking the rest of us in.

"Hello, Hedaya," my mother said. "You're looking well."

"You mean, for an old man, right?" he said, laughing.

"You look fantastic. How have you been?"

"I can't complain," he said. "My doctor says I'm healthy as a horse and business is good."

"A charmed life indeed," my mother said. "Okay, introductions. This is my daughter, Suzy."

"Oh, the bride to be," he said, shaking my hand. "You have your mother's beauty."

"Thank you," I said. "It's nice to meet you. You have a wonderful place here."

"Yes, we somehow manage to get by," he said, his eyes dancing.

"And this is Josie," my mother said. "That's Chef Claire. To her right is Millie. And on the end is Jill. That completes the bridal party."

"An amazing display of beautiful women," he said, glancing around and shaking hands with everyone. "So, are all the wedding plans finalized?"

"They better be," I whispered.

"Don't start, darling," my mother said. "Yes, we should be good to go. And I'd love it if you could be there. Gerald is flying in from Grand Cayman."

"I will do my best, but I'm still not sure if I'll be able to make it. But I would love to see Gerald. I can't believe they made that scallywag Premier," he said, laughing.

"It's probably a good time for you to put some money down there," my mother said.

"Yes, I'm sure it is," he said, nodding.

"I hope you can make it," I said. "There's plenty of room."

"Just stay at my place," my mother said. "And Summerman's band is playing at the reception."

I glanced over at Josie to gauge her reaction. She was still edgy about the prospect of seeing her former boyfriend. But her expression didn't change, and when I caught her eye, she merely shrugged it off.

"Really?" he said, surprised. "I just had them here last month for three shows."

"Ouch," my mother said. "That's a big check to write."

"Don't worry, I made it all back. What's he charging you to play at the wedding?"

"He's doing it for free," she said. "Wedding present."

"Well done," Hedaya said. "Maybe I should have had you handle my negotiations. Look, I need to run to a meeting. But I hope you'll be able to join me upstairs tonight for dinner. I'm

10

having a small dinner party and would love it if you could all be there."

My mother glanced around at all of us.

"That sounds great," I said.

Everyone else looked back and forth at each other and nodded.

"Perfect," Hedaya said. "Eight o'clock. Just take the gold elevator on the other side of the casino to the top floor." Then he beamed at us again and pulled my mother in for another hug. "It's so good to see you. Ladies, it's a pleasure meeting all of you. Enjoy your day."

I watched his brisk stride as he walked away then turned to my mother.

"Man, he's got a ton of energy. How old is he?" I said.

"I believe he just turned ninety," she said, continuing to stare after him. "He looks exactly the same as the last time I saw him."

"How does he know Summerman?"

"You know, I'm really not sure," my mother said after giving it some thought. Then she clapped her hands once. "Okay, ladies. Let the games begin. What's it going to be? An afternoon session of craps or drinks by the pool?"

"Geez, Mrs. C.," Josie deadpanned. "Not the briar patch."

Chapter 3

Chef Claire and I changed into our bathing suits and headed for the pool while the others decided to spend the afternoon in the casino after my mother offered to teach everyone how to play craps. Just before eight, freshly showered and refreshed, we headed downstairs to the main floor then walked toward a solitary gold elevator that sat on the other side of the massive floor space. Halfway across the casino, Josie glanced over at me without breaking stride.

"Quite a hike," she said.

"Yeah, I'm gonna count it," I said. "Did you win any money?"

"Fifty bucks," Josie said. "I decided to quit while I was ahead."

"Good call. How did my mother do?"

"When I left, she was up about thirty grand," Josie said, shaking her head. "She's a wild woman at the craps table."

"Where did you go after that?"

"Sportsbook," she said, shrugging. "I bet the fifty on the Blue Jays tonight."

"You come all the way to Vegas and bet baseball?" I said, frowning at her.

"What can I say? I'm a woman of simple tastes."

12

We finally reached the elevator and came face to face with an enormous bald man wearing a black suit and an earpiece. Even though it looked like he could snap a tree trunk with one hand, he beamed at us as we approached.

"Good evening, ladies," he said, glancing around. "How can I help you?"

"It's so kind of you to offer," Josie deadpanned. "There's a car outside that's got me blocked in. Would you mind moving it?"

"Don't start," I said, elbowing her gently in the ribs.

"You want me to move a car?" he said, confused.

"Yes, please. Could you just pick it up and move it over a couple spots?" Josie said with a grin.

"Good one. You know, we get a lot of comedians coming through this place," he said, fixing a friendly stare on her.

"Do you now?" she said.

"Yeah. Obviously, you're not one of them," he said.

"Harsh," Josie said, laughing.

"I'm paid to be harsh," he said, doing his best not to flirt. "What can I do for you?"

"Hedaya has invited us to dinner," my mother said, staring up at him. "Chandler. Party of six."

"Just one moment, please," he said, then talked to his sleeve and touched the earpiece. Then he gave us another smile and stepped away from the door. He slid an access card into a slot next to the elevator. The door opened and he waved us in. "Enjoy your evening."

13

The door closed behind us, and all six of us glanced around at the ornate interior as the elevator began its ascent.

"This elevator probably cost more than my house," Millie said, running a hand up and down one of the polished sides. "Do you think this is real gold?"

"I'd be surprised if it wasn't," my mother said, taking another look around.

"How much did you end up winning?" I said to my mother.

"Forty thousand," she said with a grin. "It would have been more, but I ran out of time."

"How the heck do you keep winning every time you come here?"

"I cheat," my mother said, shrugging.

"Mom!"

"I'm joking, darling," she said, giving me a coy smile.

The elevator came to a stop and opened directly into a massive living space that was, in a word, spectacular. All six of us did our best not to gawk as we stood in the foyer. A short but very attractive Asian woman approached and gave my mother a big smile.

"It's been way too long, Mrs. C," she said, extending her hand. "You look fabulous."

"It's so good to see you, Rose," my mother said, returning the handshake. "And if we're going to throw the word fabulous around, it's definitely heading in your direction."

"You're too kind," Rose said, bowing slightly before glancing around at us. "Welcome."

My mother handled the rest of the introductions then Rose beckoned for us to follow her.

"We're eating outside by the pool tonight," she said over her shoulder, then laughed. "You might want to prepare yourself. Present company excluded, Uncle has invited a rather unique collection this evening."

She led us outside to a rooftop area that appeared to be about the same size as the main floor of the casino. Again, we did our best not to gawk but failed miserably. An enormous swimming pool that looked more like a tropical island setting dominated half the space. A series of waterfalls and streams were incorporated into the overall design, and I continued to stare in disbelief at what I was seeing.

"It's nice, isn't it?" my mother said.

"You'd have to blow it up before you could call it nice, Mom. This is incredible. You've been here before?"

"I have," she said, nodding. "Actually, Paulie and I had dinner with Hedaya the last time we were in town."

"What's the deal with his niece?" I said, glancing at Rose who was chatting and laughing with the casino owner.

"Her parents were killed in China when she was a young girl, and Hedaya managed to get her smuggled out of the country. She's been with him ever since. I think she's taken over a lot of the business." Then she gently tugged my sleeve. "Let's go mingle."

We headed for the small group of people standing around Hedaya listening to a story he was telling. He finished to a big laugh and spotted my mother. He waved us over, and another round of introductions ensued. I did my best to remember the names but lost focus when I spotted the dogs. I nudged Josie and she followed my eyes.

"Well, would you look at those two?" Josie said with a big grin.

"Spaniels, right?" I said, admiring both dogs who were each tugging on one end of a long chew toy.

"Yeah. And judging by the number of Russians we were just introduced to, I'm gonna guess they're Russian spaniels."

"They're beautiful," I said.

"Thank you."

We glanced over our shoulders and saw a man giving the spaniels a loving stare.

"Sergei, right?" I said, doing my best to recall the man's name.

"You have a good memory," he said, then whistled softly. Both dogs perked up, dropped the chew toy, and trotted toward him. "Suzy and Josie, right?"

"That's right," I said, kneeling down to pet the female. "My goodness, they're gorgeous."

"Look at this guy," Josie said, sitting down on the teak deck to rub the male's head.

"You're both dog lovers," Sergei said, giving us an approving nod.

"Yeah, I guess you could say that," I said, continuing to pet the spaniel. "We run an inn for dogs at home."

"Interesting and noble work," he said, nodding. "How many dogs do you have?"

"Well, let's see," I said, trying to remember this morning's count. "Sixty-seven, not counting our four house dogs."

"Really?" he said, surprised. "That's a lot of dogs."

"Yeah, you'd think that," Josie said, shaking her head. "But not really."

That got a laugh out of him, and he glanced back and forth at us as we continued to play with the spaniels.

"What are their names?" I said.

"Moose and Squirrel."

"Moose and Squirrel?" Josie said, frowning. "Like the old Bullwinkle cartoon?"

"That's the one," he said, laughing. "I loved that show. As a Russian, I was always rooting for Boris and Natasha."

"That was a good show," I said, nodding. "Great political satire."

"Indeed," Sergei said, then focused on the male who was doing his best to pin Josie to the ground. "Easy, Moose."

"He's fine," Josie said, laughing as she struggled to stand up. "So, how do you know Hedaya?"

"I own one of the bars downstairs," he said, rubbing the male's head. "Moscow Nights."

"That's the place with the ice bar, right?" I said.

"That's it," he said. "And we're also known for our special tasting room. Basically, it's a big freezer."

"You're joking, right?" Josie said.

"Not at all. It's part of the overall experience," Sergei said. "People love sitting in there drinking Russian vodka and eating caviar."

"In a freezer?" Josie said.

"Well, it's much nicer than your basic walk-in cooler," he said, laughing. "We provide mink coats and Russian Cossack uniforms to our guests. We try to make the experience as authentic as possible. You know, my own Vegas version of War and Peace."

"Sorry, Sergei," Josie said, frowning. "I like my vodka as cold as I can get it, but that sounds a little weird."

"I'm sure you'd enjoy yourself," he said, not offended in the least. "But I'm afraid we're closed this week for some renovations."

"Well, then I guess I'll just have to drink my vodka by the pool," Josie said, grinning at him.

"Dinner is served," Rose said, approaching from behind.

We followed her to a table set for twenty, and I ended up sitting between Sergei and a Russian woman named Natalie. She was pleasant but reserved and had a dark stare that seemed to emerge every time she had a thought. Five minutes after we'd sat down, it was pretty clear she thought a lot. Across the table from me was a guy named Alexi who was somewhere in his forties with a pinkish, bloated face I attributed to copious amounts of vodka he seemed to think was water. Hedaya had introduced him earlier as a businessman from Moscow. On either side of him sat Josie and Chef Claire, and he was obviously delighted to be surrounded by my two friends. At one end of the table, my mother was sitting with Hedaya and Rose and having a great time. Millie and Jill were at the other end surrounded by a group of people I assumed were more Russians based on their accents.

"C'mon guys," Sergei said to the dogs who were obviously on the prowl for something to eat. "Moose. Squirrel. Settle."

Both dogs trotted over to him then stretched out under the table at his feet.

"They're well-behaved," I said to Sergei.

"Yes, they're great dogs," he said, reaching down to pet their heads.

"So, what's the deal with Natalie?" I whispered, leaning in close to him.

"Ostensibly, she's a fashion designer," Sergei whispered back.

"Ostensibly?"

"Actually, she's a spy," he whispered in my ear.

19

"Really?" I said, sneaking a peek at the deep frown she was displaying.

"Yes," he said with a casual shrug.

"What's she doing here?"

"My best guess is that she's keeping an eye on Alexi," he said, nodding at the businessman who was laughing at something Josie had said.

"Okay," I said. "What's he doing?"

"He probably wants to hide some of his ill-gotten gains and is hoping Hedaya might be willing to help him," Sergei said.

"Ill-gotten gains, huh? You make it sound so mysterious."

"No, there really wasn't anything mysterious about it," he said, shrugging. "As soon as Alexi got permission, he went in and took it."

"He needed permission?"

"In my country, you need permission to do pretty much everything. Especially when it comes to money."

"What did he take?" I said, glancing across the table at the businessman who was now sharing a laugh with Chef Claire.

"Oil."

"I assume he took a lot of it," I said.

"He took all of it," Natalie said.

I flinched when I heard the thick accent of the alleged spy sitting to my left. I glanced over at her.

"Have you been eavesdropping, Natalie?" Sergei said with a chuckle.

20

"What can I say, Sergei?" she said. "It's what I do."

For a spy, she didn't seem very concerned about who knew it. And since I have a certain fondness for snooping, I couldn't resist the chance to see if she might be willing to share a few tips.

"Are you really a spy?" I whispered to her.

"Formerly," she said, shrugging. "I'm retired."

That got a snort out of Sergei, and Natalie leaned forward and glared at him.

"You have something to say, Sergei?"

"No, Natalie," he said, grinning at her. "Retired. You're funny."

Not a word I would use to describe her, but I was intrigued.

"That sounds fascinating," I said, leaning closer. "You must have a bunch of cool gadgets."

"Gadgets?" she said, frowning at me.

"Yeah, you know, all sorts of equipment you use when you're doing your...surveillance work."

"Why do you ask? Are you somehow involved in the business?" she said, still giving me a quizzical look.

"Nah, I'm just a fan," I said, taking a sip of wine. "I'd ask for details, but if you told me, you'd probably have to kill me, right?"

"What?" she said, staring at me in disbelief.

"That's okay," I said, shaking my head. "Forget I even asked."

"So, how is the bar business, Sergei?" the oil thief said in a booming voice.

"It's quite good, Alexi," Sergei said, glancing across the table. "Unfortunately, Moscow Nights is closed for renovations this week."

"Oh, that's too bad," Alexi said, tossing back a shot of vodka. "I was hoping to spend some time in your freezer."

"You do look good in a Cossack uniform," Sergei said, raising his glass in salute.

"Yes, I do, don't I?" Alexi said with a loud laugh.

"You're the owner of Moscow Nights?" Chef Claire said to Sergei.

"Yes, I am," he said, nodding with pride.

"I'd love to get a look at how you set up your tasting room," she said. "The ice bar sounds amazing."

"I have two of them. They're like small hockey rinks," he said with a shrug. "The technology is very similar."

"I'm so disappointed the bar is closed at the moment," Chef Claire said.

"If you would like to swing by during the day, I'd be happy to arrange a tour. If you don't mind being surrounded by a construction crew."

"Not at all," she said, grinning at me. "I'm quite used to it these days."

I knew she was referring to the chaos we were still dealing with at home as construction on our new animal rescue center continued. Chef Claire was right. We were all getting used to the

22

noisy mess and the amount of time it was taking to finish, but we were definitely looking forward to it being done.

"Just stop by whenever you like," Sergei said. "I'll be there all day."

"I think I'll do that," Chef Claire said.

Hedaya got to his feet to address his dinner guests. He topped off the champagne glasses near him then refilled his own and raised it.

"A toast to new friends," he said. "May the friends you make tonight be long and lasting."

The rest of us clinked glasses and drank.

"My chef will be out shortly to explain what we're having," Hedaya continued. "Eat well, my friends."

Then he sat back down and resumed the conversation he was having with my mother and his niece.

"A man of few words," Natalie said, glancing across the table at the oil thief. "What a welcome change."

I watched as a line of servers approached the table carrying silver trays. The plates were covered, and I stared down at mine like a three-year-old dying to open a Christmas present. Josie was also focused on hers and obviously fighting the urge to sneak a peek. Then a tall man dressed in white wearing a chef's hat strolled toward the table. Chef Claire shrieked and jumped to her feet.

"Louie!"

23

"Chef Claire?" he said, giving her a warm embrace. "What the heck are you doing here?"

"Girls getaway," she said, gesturing at us. "How long has it been?"

"I haven't seen you since we left culinary school," he said, then focused. "Let's catch up later after I finish work."

"Absolutely," she said, sitting back down with an enormous grin.

"I'd like to welcome all of you," Louie said, sliding his hat back in place. "I think you'll enjoy tonight's meal in this wonderful rooftop setting."

Then he nodded at the servers who continued to stand behind us. They removed the silver covers from the dinner plates then stepped back.

"We're starting tonight with Banh Cuon, a Vietnamese pork dumpling mixed with shallots and garlic and a few other special ingredients I'm suddenly not willing to share," Louie said, laughing as he glanced at Chef Claire.

"Like I need to steal your recipes," Chef Claire said, laughing along.

"Enjoy," Louie said, taking a small bow. "We'll be back soon with the next course."

We watched him wave to Chef Claire then head back to the kitchen.

"I can't believe it," Chef Claire said, shaking her head.

"He's been my personal chef for three years," Hedaya said. "What a coincidence."

"He's an amazing chef," Chef Claire said.

"One of the best I've ever seen," Hedaya said.

"Wait until you taste *her* food," my mother said, nodding at Chef Claire.

"You're so sweet, Mrs. C."

"This dumpling is incredible," I said through a mouthful then caught the look my mother was giving me. "Sorry, Mom," I said with a shrug. Then I glanced over at Natalie who was making short work of her first course. "So, Natalie. What kind of camera do you use?"

"Camera?" she said, frowning at me.

"Yeah, you know, the camera you use for surveillance and stuff like that."

"If I need to take a picture, I just use my phone," she said, not looking up from her dumpling.

"Oh," I said, disappointed.

25

Chapter 4

After dinner, Josie and I took Hedaya up on his offer to give us a tour of the rooftop. My mother, along with Millie and Jill, headed back down to the casino to play craps, while Chef Claire remained poolside to catch up with her friend from culinary school. I barely managed to keep pace with the ninety-year-old as he led us past the waterfalls at the far end of the pool and through a set of automatic doors that opened onto a massive atrium. A polished teak path stretched out in front of us, and after only a few steps, we found ourselves standing in what had to be the world's largest man-made rainforest. As we strolled along the winding path, we paid close attention as he pointed out various plants and flowers and did our best not to stare.

"This is incredible, Hedaya," Josie said, staring straight up at the glass ceiling that must have been sixty feet high. "But wasn't building a rainforest on the top of your casino a bit eccentric?"

"We're in Vegas," he said with a small shrug.

"Fair point," Josie said, nodding.

"And it's certainly no more eccentric than the curling rink I built in the basement," he said, beaming as he glanced back and forth at us.

"Well, it's your money, right?" I said, taking another look around.

26

"Whatever I don't have to give to the government," he said, laughing.

"Can I ask you a question?" I said.

"Of course."

"What's the deal with all the Russians?"

"Oh, that," he said. "They're friends and associates who just happened to be in town at the same time. So, I thought it would be nice to have them all over for dinner. What's the matter? Do you have a problem with Russians?"

"Not at all. In fact, I think they're the first ones I've ever met," I said. "And Sergei is very nice. How long has he had his vodka bar in the casino?"

"It's coming up on five years," Hedaya said, coming to a stop as we approached a fork in the path. "I thought he was crazy when he first broached the idea with me. I mean, who would want to sit in a freezer wearing a Cossack uniform, right?"

"It's not high on my list," Josie said, glancing around.

"Turns out I was very wrong," he said. "He's doing very well."

"Is Natalie really a spy?" I whispered.

"I'm sure she is," he said, then frowned as he gave it some thought. "Or at least she was. Or is trying to get out. I can never keep her situation straight."

"Doesn't it bother you to know that you have a spy hanging around your casino?" I said, finding his casual response a bit odd.

27

"Actually, it would bother me a lot more if I didn't," he said, grinning at me.

"Sure, sure."

"C'mon, follow me," Hedaya said, taking the path on the right. "There's someone I want you to meet."

Josie glanced at me as we followed him, and I shrugged back. We walked until a glass wall appeared on our left that ran for several hundred feet. It was about ten feet high, and Hedaya kept peering inside as he walked then stopped and glanced at us.

"He must be hiding tonight," he said, then took another look.

"Who's hiding?" I said, peering through the thick glass.

"Bugsy," he said.

"Bugsy, as in Seigel?" I said, remembering the name of the famous mobster.

"His namesake," Hedaya said, nodding.

"A pet?" I said, frowning.

"No, I wouldn't actually call him a pet," Hedaya said. "But over the years, Bugsy has gotten quite tame."

"Snake?" I said, fearing the worst.

"No. Komodo Dragon," Hedaya said, beaming at us.

I stared at him in disbelief then looked at Josie who was also having a hard time processing what the old man had just told us.

"You have a Komodo Dragon?" Josie said, giving him a wide-eyed stare.

"Yes, I do."

"And you built this glass enclosure just for him?" I said.

"I did. And the rainforest," he said, nodding. "Several years ago. Right after I got him as a gift from the President of Indonesia."

"Should I even ask?" I said to Josie.

"Sure, why not?" she said, laughing.

"The President was very appreciative of the money I gave to an institute established to keep the Dragons from going extinct," Hedaya said, not waiting for the question. "He decided to give me one as a thank you as long as I agreed to take good care of him."

"Those things get huge," Josie said, peering through the glass enclosure. "Up to ten feet, right?"

"Well, Bugsy is a bit of a freak of nature," he said, rocking back and forth on his heels. "Several museums have already contacted me about putting him on display after he passes. Hopefully, that is something I won't have to worry about for several years."

"Okay," I said, scowling. "How big is he?"

"Thirteen feet," Hedaya said. "At least he was the last time we measured him. He bit the guy holding the tape measure, so we decided to quit worrying about it. Bugsy doesn't like to have his measurements taken."

"Was the guy okay?" I said. "Their bite can be poisonous."

"Eventually," Hedaya said. "Now, we pretty much leave Bugsy alone. But he is fun to watch. He has a ton of personality. A truly unique creature. And in case you haven't figured it out yet, I'm someone with a penchant for the unique."

29

"I gotta see this lizard," Josie said, laughing.

"He must be on the other end," Hedaya said, motioning for us to follow him.

We resumed walking, then all three of us froze in our tracks when we spotted the body spread out on the ground inside the enclosure.

"What on earth?" Hedaya said, blinking several times.

"It's Sergei," I said, staring at my dinner companion. "He's foaming at the mouth."

"I'm afraid that's all he's going to be doing," Josie said as she peered through the glass at the body sprawled on the ground.

"Dead?" Hedaya said, glancing at her.

"Yeah, I'm pretty sure," Josie said. "But there's only one way to find out." Then she looked at me and deadpanned, "Go check it out, Suzy."

"Yeah, right," I said. "Like I'm going to get in there with a thirteen-foot lizard."

"Hang on," Hedaya said, reaching for his phone. "Let me call security."

"Wait a sec," Josie said, placing a hand on his arm then pointing at something emerging from the shadows.

"Geez, look at the size of him," I said, staring in disbelief at the lizard slowly lumbering toward us.

"There's something wrong," Hedaya said.

"You mean apart from the dead Russian?" Josie said.

30

"It's Bugsy," he said, studying the lizard closely. "What on earth is the matter with him?"

"It looks like the poor guy is choking on something," Josie said, focused intently on the massive creature on the other side of the glass wall.

We watched the lizard desperately trying to catch its breath as it lurched up and down on its front legs shaking its head.

"I've got to get a veterinarian over here," Hedaya said, frantic.

"It's your lucky day, Hedaya," Josie said.

"You're a vet?" he said, staring at her.

"I am," she said. "But I'm going to need a whole bunch of help handling that thing."

"Of course," he said, focusing on his phone. "Charlie. Come to the rainforest now. And bring at least two more guys with you."

"Tell them to stop by our suite first. 3112," Josie said. "My medical bag is on the dresser. The first bedroom on the right."

"You brought your bag with you?" Hedaya said, bewildered.

"I never travel without it," she said, shrugging. "You never know when you're going to have to save the life of a prehistoric lizard, right?"

Hedaya shook his head but completed the call. Then he focused on the lizard that continued to emit sounds I'd never heard before.

"They should be here in just a few minutes," Hedaya said, staring at the lizard. "I hope he can hang on."

31

"How are you gonna do this?" I said to Josie.

"That, my friend, is a very good question," she said, taking a few steps forward until she was right across from the struggling monitor. "But as soon as Hedaya's guys get hold of him, I'm definitely starting with sedation."

"What are you gonna use?" I said.

"Acepromazine," she said. "It's the only one I've got with me."

"How much sedative are you going to use?" Hedaya said.

"A lot," Josie said with another shrug. Then she noticed the concerned look on the old man's face and placed a hand on his forearm. "Don't worry, Hedaya. I'll figure it out."

"Have you ever worked on lizards before?" he said.

"Sure, but nothing like the size of that guy."

While we waited for security, I kept glancing back and forth between the choking lizard and the dead Russian.

"This is going to put a damper on our plans, huh?" Josie said, forcing a small laugh.

"Don't worry about that," I said, then nodded at the lizard that was obviously fighting for its life. "Just try and save the poor thing."

Three security people, led by the guy who'd been outside the gold elevator downstairs raced along the path and came to a stop next to Hedaya. Josie grabbed her work bag from one of the guards. Trying to process what they were looking at, the security staff focused on Hedaya.

32

"It appears that Sergei is dead," Hedaya said, doing his best to stay calm. "But check him out to be sure when you go in, Charlie. You two need to get hold of Bugsy so Josie can work on him."

"You want us to grab the lizard?" one of the men said, glancing through the glass.

"Well, I certainly don't want you to stand around and watch him choke to death," Hedaya snapped.

"I'm not sure three guys will be enough," the other security guard said.

"I'll help you," I said.

"Are you nuts?" Josie said.

"Probably," I said, following the men to the entrance. Then I called out to them. "I get the tail."

Hedaya slid an access card into the slot, and I followed everyone inside the glass enclosure and hung back waiting for Josie's instructions. I glanced at the Russian sprawled out on the ground and was pretty sure Sergei was dead. The lizard continued to hack and shake its head as it bounced up and down on its front feet.

"How the heck are we going to do this?" one of the security people said.

"Two of you need to get your arms around his neck and keep his head still," Josie said, filling a syringe.

"Are you out of your mind?" he said. "That thing could bite my face off."

33

"What do you think I'm going to do to you if he dies?" Hedaya said in a tone that made the hairs on the back of my neck stand up.

"When you grab him, he's gonna get cranky in a hurry," Josie said. "Suzy, you head for his tail and do everything you can to keep it steady. The other guy needs to grab one of his front legs and lift it off the ground. When I say the word, all of you need to work together and do everything you can to flip him over onto his back in one motion."

"That's your plan?" one of the security guards said, staring at her.

"You got a better idea?" Josie said, glaring at him.

"No," he whispered. "Okay, let's get this over with."

I raced for the lizard's tail and knelt down behind it. Given its struggles, the lizard, while aware of our presence, remained primarily focused on trying to catch its breath. Charlie knelt down over Sergei's body then got to his feet and took up his position near the lizard's head. He looked up at Hedaya who was standing nearby.

"Sergei's definitely dead," he said.

Hedaya nodded then stared at the lizard that was quickly running out of steam. The security guards moved as a unit and grabbed the lizard that tried to protest with snapping jowls but was severely hampered by its lack of air. I straddled the tail and waited for further instructions.

"Okay," Josie said, raising the syringe. "Flip him over."

Everyone lifted, and the lizard eventually went over onto its back and kicked its legs in protest. I gave the tail room to turn over then used my knees for support and pressed down hard with both hands.

"Hang in there, Bugsy," Josie said, dropping to her knees and inching the syringe underneath the lizard's neck. "You're gonna take a nice long nap."

Then the lizard managed to get one of his front feet loose and dragged its claws over Josie's left wrist and forearm. She let loose with an impressive string of expletives as she took a quick look at the damage the claws had done. Then she injected the lizard with the sedative. Soon, the lizard stopped struggling, and its distress calls began to soften.

"Are you okay?" I said, staring at the stream of blood pouring out of Josie's arm.

"Yeah," she said, putting the syringe back in her bag then pressing her hand against the wound. "But he got me pretty good. I'm gonna need some stitches."

"I'll call for a doctor," Hedaya said, reaching for his phone. "Are you still going to be able to do the surgery?"

"Sure," she said, shrugging. "I just need to wrap it. There should be a roll of gauze in my bag."

Hedaya found it and spent a few minutes wrapping the wound until the flow of blood was minimized. Josie stared down at the lizard until the sedative had taken full effect then nodded.

"Okay, he shouldn't be moving around much," Josie said, kneeling down next to the lizard. "But keep a tight hold of his head and tail just in case."

"What are you going to do?" Hedaya said, kneeling next to her.

"I'm going to go in through Bugsy's esophagus," she said calmly. "The way he was moving his head and the sound he was making tells me he's got something stuck in there that's partially blocking his breathing."

"Only partially?" Hedaya said.

"Yeah, if it was a complete blockage, he'd be dead by now," she said, reaching into her bag.

I spent the next few minutes straddling the thirteen-foot lizard's tail staring in disbelief as I watched Josie meticulously slice open the lizard's skin under its neck, then shine a small flashlight. She continued to wipe the blood away from the opening as she peered inside the lizard's throat. Then she shook her head and reached for an instrument that looked like a large pair of tweezers.

"What the heck?" she said, removing a bloody gold key from the lizard. She dropped the key in Hedaya's hand then immediately went back to work sewing the opening shut.

"A key?" Hedaya said, staring in disbelief as he wiped the blood off it.

"What kind of key is it?" I said.

36

"It looks like a key to a safe-deposit box," Hedaya said. "It must have fallen out of Sergei's pocket."

"Not the smartest thing to eat," Josie said, not looking up from her stitch work. "He somehow managed to get it wedged in there. Poor guy."

She spent several minutes closing the wound with a concentrated stare. The lizard occasionally twitched and tried to move around, but the four of us kept him pinned in place.

"Is he going to be okay?" Hedaya said, leaning forward to watch Josie work.

"Well, he's probably going to be off his food for a few days," she said, eventually sitting down and tossing her instruments back in the bag. "But I don't see why he won't be just fine."

"That was amazing work," Hedaya said, beaming at her. "I can't thank you enough."

"No problem," she said, climbing to her feet and brushing herself off. "Buy me a burger and a beer, and we'll call it even."

"That I can do," he said, placing a hand on her shoulder. "I need to get in touch with the police about Sergei. Let's head back outside and get you stitched up.

"Yeah, that's probably a good idea," she said, glancing at her arm. "And while he's out, you might want to clip his nails."

"You're joking, right?" Hedaya said, cocking his head at her.

"Yes, Hedaya," she said, laughing. "I'm joking." Then she turned to us. "Let's get him flipped back over so he doesn't freak out when he comes to."

37

We eventually got the lizard turned over then I brushed myself off and headed for Josie who continued to examine the deep gouge on her lower arm.

"Great job," I said, giving her a hug. "Maybe we can open a lizard surgery center on the side."

"No, I think I'll stick with dogs," she said, shaking her head. "Well, you did promise me a memorable weekend."

"Yes, I did. And we're just getting started," I said, glancing over at the dead Russian.

"That's what I'm afraid of."

Chapter 5

We left the rainforest and headed back to the pool area where Chef Claire was still chatting with Louie. When she saw the bloody bandage on Josie's arm, she got to her feet, obviously concerned.

"What the heck happened to you?" she said, gently holding Josie's hand for a closer look.

"You wouldn't believe it if I told you," Josie said.

"Try me," Chef Claire said, staring at her.

"I got gouged by a thirteen-foot-long Komodo Dragon."

"Okay, fine," Chef Claire snapped. "Don't tell me."

I laughed and extended my hand to the chef who was standing next to her.

"Hi, Louie. I'm Suzy. It's nice to meet you."

"Same here," he said, returning the handshake. "Chef Claire has been talking about you guys nonstop."

"Yeah, she does get chatty when she drinks," I said.

"What a great idea. Let's all sit down and enjoy a cocktail," Hedaya said, gesturing at the now empty dinner table.

We followed him and got settled in. He made a call and a couple of servers carrying ice buckets filled with bottles of champagne soon arrived. Moments later, a man carrying a medical bag approached the table and shook hands with Hedaya.

39

"How are you doing, Hedaya?" he said, glancing at the bandage on Josie's arm.

"I'm fine, Doc. And thanks for coming over at this time of night. We need you to do a bit of sewing on my friend."

"What happened?" the doctor said, pulling up a chair and sitting down next to Josie.

"Bugsy had a bit of problem and Josie saved his life," Hedaya said, beaming at her.

"Who's Bugsy?" Chef Claire said.

"He's my Komodo Dragon," Hedaya said.

"Really?" she said, baffled.

He nodded. Chef Claire looked at Josie.

"Sorry."

"Don't worry about it," Josie said. "I wouldn't have believed it either."

"That is one nasty cut," the doctor said after removing the bloody gauze. "You're gonna need a whole bunch of stitches."

"Yeah, he got me good," Josie said, glancing down at the scratches. "Knock yourself out, Doc."

"You're pretty calm about it," the doctor said.

"Occupational hazard," she said, shrugging it off.

"You're a vet?"

"I am."

"What happened to the lizard?" he said, filling a syringe.

"He ate something that didn't agree with him," Josie said, glancing up at two people approaching the table.

Hedaya followed her eyes and spotted them. He got to his feet.

"If you'll excuse me for a few minutes, I need to escort the police to the rainforest."

"Rainforest?" Chef Claire said, again baffled.

"Yeah, it's amazing," I said. "They're going to check Sergei out."

"Who the heck is Sergei?"

"The dead Russian."

"Sergei is dead?" Louie said, stunned by the news.

"Yeah," I said, nodding.

"The guy you were sitting next to at dinner?" Chef Claire said.

"That's the one," I said.

"What happened to him?" Louie said.

"I don't know," I said, shaking my head. "We didn't have a chance to take a close look. We were a little busy dealing with the choking lizard."

"Male strippers are going to be a letdown after this," Josie deadpanned, then flinched. "Hey, Doc. You can skip the needlepoint, just sew it up."

"Sorry," he said, reaching for the syringe and applying more local anesthetic. "Let's just give that a few seconds."

One of the servers made her way to Josie to take her order.

"I'd like a bacon cheeseburger and a Molson Ale. Thanks."

41

"Of course," the server said, scribbling it down and moving on.

"You just ate dinner an hour and a half ago," I said, staring at her in disbelief.

"What can I say?" she said, shrugging. "Performing emergency surgery on giant lizards always makes me hungry."

I shook my head at her then spotted Hedaya making his way back. He sat down next to me and helped himself to a glass of champagne.

"What do the cops have to say?" I said, taking a sip.

"Not much yet. They said they'll give me an update as soon as they finish their initial review," he said, shaking his head. "Their first guess is some sort of poison."

"Maybe he came face to face with Bugsy and had a heart attack," I said, half-serious.

"I suppose that's possible," Hedaya said, frowning. "He certainly does get your attention."

"But how the heck did he get inside the enclosure?" I said. "Did Sergei have an access card?"

"No, he didn't," Hedaya said. "There are only two of those. I have one, and the other is assigned to the person responsible for taking care of Bugsy. Sergei must have climbed in."

"Climbed in? That glass wall must be ten feet high."

"It is odd," he said, scowling.

"Was Sergei involved in anything you might consider…nefarious?" I said, casting my line out.

"Up until an hour ago, I would have said no," Hedaya said. "Now, I'm not so sure."

"What did the cops have to say about the key?"

"Oh, I didn't tell the cops about the key," Hedaya said, shaking his head.

"Because you don't know what might be inside whatever that key opens, right?"

Hedaya studied the look on my face then gave me a grin.

"Your mother has told me about your powers of deduction."

"Yeah, I have my moments."

Then an idea floated to the surface and I frowned.

"What's wrong?" Hedaya said.

"Does Sergei have any family here?" I said.

"No, he's always been a committed bachelor. Why do you ask?"

"I'm wondering what's going to happen to his dogs."

"Oh, the dogs," Hedaya said.

"If you don't mind," I said, downing the last of my champagne. "We'll be more than happy to keep an eye on them while we're here."

Chapter 6

After one more glass of champagne, Josie and I headed back to our suite with the spaniels after promising to stay awake until the two detectives showed up to ask what I was sure would be a lengthy list of questions. Chef Claire remained poolside with her friend from culinary school, and the rest of the gang were still downstairs playing craps. We opened the sliding glass doors and stepped outside onto the balcony that offered a magnificent view of the Strip and stretched out on lounge chairs. Moose, the male, hopped up on Josie's chair and draped himself across her chest. Squirrel did the same with me before finally settling down near my feet. After staring out at the lights and the dark desert landscape for several minutes, I glanced over at Josie who was also watching the night sky deep in thought.

"That was incredible," I said.

"The bacon cheeseburger?"

"No, not the burger," I said, making a face at her. "What you did for that lizard. How did you know what to do?"

"I think it was a combination of paying just enough attention in class and a splash of good luck."

"Luck?" I said, shaking my head. "I doubt if that had anything to do with it."

"Well, we are in Vegas," Josie said, glancing over at me.

"Fair point. Maybe you should start playing downstairs."

44

"I'd rather do another surgery on Bugsy," she said, frowning at the possibility of giving away any of her hard-earned money. "Did you get a chance to call the Inn?"

"I did," I said, stifling a yawn. "Everything is fine. And Sammy invited all the guys over to the house to play cards and smoke cigars."

"Out on the deck, right?" Josie said, raising an eyebrow.

"I told him that if we picked up a trace of cigar smoke in the house, he'd be on poop-patrol for a month."

"That oughta do it," she said, glancing back out at the night sky. "How do you want to spend the day tomorrow?"

"It depends," I said, making room for Squirrel who was restless and needing some attention. She nestled against my chest and I rubbed her head. "Definitely some time at the pool. Maybe check out the old downtown area. But I want to wait until we hear what the cops have to say."

"Of course," Josie said with a heavy sigh. "We can't decide how to spend your bachelorette weekend until we talk to the cops."

"It does kinda sound backward, doesn't it?" I said, laughing. "You know, usually you talk to the cops after."

"Yeah," she said, shaking her head. "Just promise me you'll be careful, Suzy. This is obviously some sort of Russian situation. And the guy I sat next to at dinner is definitely a heavy hitter. He couldn't resist telling Chef Claire and me that he's worth billions."

"According to Sergei, he made it by stealing as many oil rights as he could get his hands on," I said, giving Squirrel a tummy rub after she rolled over in my lap.

"How the heck did he get away with that?"

"Apparently, he had permission."

"He had permission to steal Russian oil?" she said, sitting up on the lounger.

"Yeah."

"You know what that means."

"That this guy Alexi is well-connected with the Russian government?" I said, glancing over.

"I'm no expert, but I imagine you have to be well-connected over there just to *buy* oil. If he had permission to steal it and make billions in the process, this guy is joined at the hip with you know who."

"I'm sure he is," I said, nodding as I stared back out at the neon display.

"Which makes him a very dangerous guy to be around much less mess with," Josie said, her voice rising in warning. "So, just let the cops do their job. We'll spend our time doing fun things."

"I don't think the cops are going to be able to piece everything together," I whispered.

"Oh, here we go," she said, shaking her head. "Why not?"

"Remember the key you pulled out of Bugsy's throat?"

"What about it?"

"Hedaya didn't mention it to the cops," I said.

46

Josie stroked Moose's head as she pondered the implications of my comment.

"You think the old man is involved with those people?"

"Well, the dead guy did run the vodka bar downstairs," I said, shrugging. "And there had to be at least a dozen Russians at dinner tonight. Including Alexi and the spy sitting next to me."

"Natasha, right?" Josie said, frowning.

"No, Natalie."

"Sorry. I must have been extending the Bullwinkle reference," she said, laughing.

"Moose and Squirrel," I said in my best Russian accent. Both dogs perked up for a second, then settled back down on the loungers. "But why would Hedaya need to get mixed up with people like that? According to my mom, he's a billionaire."

"Suzy, the guy built a rainforest on the top of his casino just so his Komodo Dragon would have a nice place to live. In my book, that's the sign of an eccentric with way too much money on his hands. It's really not much of a stretch to consider the possibility that he might be involved in all sorts of unsavory activities."

"I suppose you're right," I said, then paused when I heard the knock on the door.

"Did you order room service?" Josie said, glancing inside.

"No," I said, getting up and heading for the door. "That's a cop knock."

Chapter 7

I opened the door and found a man and a woman standing outside with blank stares on their faces. I glanced at the female detective first, and she gave me a hint of a smile. Then it disappeared and I looked at the other cop. He seemed very familiar, and I must have been frowning because he swallowed the last of what he'd been eating and the look on his face turned from casual to a questioning scowl that bordered on hostile.

"What's the matter?" the male detective said, brushing both sides of his face searching for food remnants or a trail of mustard.

"It's nothing," I said, shaking my head. "You just look very familiar. Have we met?"

"I don't believe so," he said, relaxing a bit. "Are you Ms. Chandler?"

"I am."

"This is Detective Swan," he said, nodding at his partner. "And I'm Detective Williams. May we come in?"

"Of course," I said, motioning them inside the suite. "Have a seat. Can I get you something to drink?"

"No, we're fine," he said, sitting down on a couch. Detective Swan sat down next to him and flipped to a fresh page in her notebook. "We finished our interviews upstairs, but we have a few questions for you and Ms. Court."

48

"I'm right here," Josie said, entering the suite trailed by both dogs. She sat down in a chair across from the detectives and got comfortable. "And call me Josie."

"Okay…Josie," he said, doing his best not to stare at her.

I slid into another chair and Squirrel immediately hopped up on my lap. I groaned softly when she landed on my stomach and waited patiently until the spaniel got settled down.

"Now, Ms. Chandler," he said, glancing down at his notebook.

"Suzy," I said, again staring at him. "Are you sure we haven't met?"

"He does look familiar," Josie said, glancing over at me.

"Yeah, it's driving me crazy," I said, staring at the detective.

"I'm sure I would have remembered if we had met," he said, responding to me but looking at Josie. Then the penny dropped and he turned his head and stared at me in disbelief. "Suzy Chandler?"

"Yeah, what about it?" I said, suddenly on the defensive.

"From Clay Bay?"

"Yes," I whispered.

"I don't believe it," he said, glancing at his partner.

"Clay Bay?" Detective Swan said, frowning. "Isn't that where your brother is stationed?"

"That's the place," Detective Williams said. "*You're* Suzy Chandler?"

49

"And you're the brother of the Detective Williams who works for the state police," I said, shaking my head in disbelief. "I can't believe it."

"Wow," Josie said. "Small world, huh?"

"My brother has been telling me stories about this woman you wouldn't believe," he said, laughing as he looked at Detective Swan.

"Like what?" I said, now testy.

The detective in question and I had crossed swords several times in the past over my inability to keep my nose out of police work he considered none of my business. I thought we had come to an understanding based on mutual respect and negotiated boundaries. Apparently, I was wrong. I needed to hear exactly what he'd been saying to his brother who held a similar position here in Vegas.

"Oh, he's just been telling me about your inability to let the police handle situations that fall inside their jurisdiction," he said with a smirk I so wanted to knock off his face. "I believe the term he used was an uncontrollable inquisitiveness."

"Really? He said that about me?" I said, glaring at him. "I can't believe it."

Josie snorted.

"Shut it," I snapped, then focused on the detective. "Did he also tell you about how many cases I've helped him solve?"

"Actually, no. He did not," Detective Williams said with a casual shrug.

"Then the next time you guys talk, you might want to ask him," I said, running both hands along the spaniel's fur to calm myself down. "So, tell me, Detective Williams, does pompous arrogance run in the family or is that personality trait confined to your brother?"

"Uh, Suzy?" Josie said, glancing over at me.

"What?"

"Dial it down," she said calmly. "Just let the detectives do their job. You can save the hostility for Detective William's brother when we get home."

"I can't believe he's been badmouthing me," I said.

"He really hasn't been doing that," the detective said. "It's more of a general observation about your overall personality. Actually, I think he's quite fond of you."

"Yeah, I bet," I said, forcing myself to relax. "Okay, why don't you ask your questions?"

"What a good idea," Detective Swan said, leaning forward. "We understand that you both had dinner with Hedaya on the rooftop earlier this evening."

"We did," Josie said.

"And after dinner, while Hedaya was giving you a tour of his rooftop rainforest you discovered the body of a man named Sergei Kastakovitch inside the glass enclosure where a thirteen-foot Komodo Dragon resides," she said, then glanced at her partner. "Did that sound as strange as I think it did?"

51

"Yeah, it's definitely a weird one," Detective Williams said, shaking his head.

"Yes, we did," I said. "Hedaya was about to introduce us to Bugsy when we found the body."

"Okay," Detective Williams said, glancing down at his notes. "What happened after that?"

"Before Hedaya could open the enclosure, we saw Bugsy, and it was obvious he was having trouble breathing," Josie said. "So, it quickly became apparent that the lizard was going to need some help."

"And you're the one who provided that help, correct?" Detective Swan said.

"Yes. Hedaya called his security team and they swung by here to pick up my medical bag," Josie said, nodding. "When they arrived at the rainforest, we came up with a plan to immobilize the lizard. When that was done, I administered a sedative, and as soon as it took effect, I performed emergency surgery to remove a blockage from the lizard's throat."

"What sort of blockage was it?" Detective Williams said.

Josie paused, then glanced at me before answering.

"I'm not exactly sure," she said, lying through her teeth. "It was very bloody and I immediately handed it to Hedaya. Then I went back to work sewing up the incision. How did Hedaya describe it?"

"A piece of metal," Detective Swan said, checking her notes.

"That sounds about right," Josie said, nodding. "The lizard must have found it on the ground and tried to eat it. It got lodged in its throat."

"But what about the body?" Detective Williams said.

"What about it?" I said.

"Did anyone check on the condition of Mr. Kastakovitch before you dealt with the lizard's breathing problem?" Detective Swan said, glancing back and forth at both of us.

"Yes," I said. "Hedaya instructed his head of security to do that first before he helped the rest of us get control of the lizard. I remember him telling Hedaya that Sergei was definitely dead."

"Okay," Detective Williams said, scribbling into his notebook. "Who else was at dinner this evening?"

"Just our group and a bunch of Russians," I said with a shrug.

"Yes, we're aware of that," he said. "Which ones?"

"Didn't Hedaya already tell you that?" I said.

"He did," Detective Williams said. "We're just trying to confirm who was there."

"Well, let's see," I said, trying to remember who'd been sitting where. "On the end of the table to my left were Hedaya and his niece."

"Rose, right?" Detective Swan said.

"Yes. And my mother was sitting between them."

"And where is your mother at the moment?" Detective Williams said.

53

"She's downstairs playing craps with two other women who made the trip with us."

"Millie and Jill," Josie said, making room on the overstuffed chair for Moose who wanted some attention.

"They headed down to the casino right after dinner," I said. "Given the number of cameras around, you shouldn't have any problems confirming that."

"Yeah, thanks for the tip," Detective Williams deadpanned as he rolled his eyes at his partner.

"So, it does run in the family," I said.

"Knock...it...off," Josie whispered.

"Who else was at the table?" Detective Swan said, doing her best to keep the conversation on track.

"Well, I was sitting between Sergei and a woman named Natalie. Apparently, she works in the fashion industry," I said. "Across from me were Josie and Chef Claire who were sitting on either side of a man named Alexi."

"Chef Claire?" Detective Williams said, checking his notes.

"She's the one who was talking with Hedaya's personal chef next to the pool," Detective Swan said.

"That's right," he said, then looked at me. "This Chef Claire is the other member of your party?"

"She is," I said. "There are six of us here for the weekend. My bachelorette party."

"Congratulations," Detective Swan said, finally smiling. "When's the wedding?"

54

"Next month," I said, then glanced at the other detective. "And your brother is coming."

"Yes, he mentioned he was going to a wedding," Detective Williams said. "He's looking forward to it."

"He might not be after I put him at one of the kids' tables," I whispered.

Josie snorted then started scratching Moose's ears.

"What?" he said.

"Nothing," I said, shaking my head. Then I thought about the others who'd been at dinner. "At the other end of the table, Millie and Jill were sitting with a bunch of other Russians I didn't get a chance to talk to."

"You were sitting next to the man named Alexi?" Detective Swan said to Josie.

"I was. I don't know him," she said. "But he was a good dinner companion. He seems to be an interesting guy."

"How so?" the female detective said.

"He had a lot of good stories," Josie said. "And a ton of personality. I'm sure you picked up on that when you interviewed him."

"Actually, we haven't had a chance to speak to him," Detective Swan said. "He disappeared right after dinner."

"Well, I'm sure he's around somewhere," Josie said with a shrug.

"Yes, that's our hope," Detective Williams said to himself more than anyone else. "Are these the victim's dogs?"

55

"They are," I said. "We're going to watch them for the rest of the weekend and then see what happens."

"You'll try to find a good home for them?" Detective Swan said.

"Oh, they've already found a good home," I said, stroking the female's back. "We'll be looking around to see if there's a better one for them."

"I don't like our chances," Josie said, grinning at me.

"Yeah, me either."

"Okay, I think we're just about done here," Detective Williams said, glancing down at his notebook. "Just one more question. While you were in the rainforest did you see anything out of the ordinary?"

"You mean, apart from the dead Russian and the choking thirteen-foot lizard, right?" Josie deadpanned.

"Yes, apart from that."

"Not really," Josie said, then frowned. "But at one point, I thought I did hear some rustling in the bushes."

"While you were performing the surgery?" Detective Swan said.

"Yeah. I didn't give it much thought at the time," she said.

"Why not?" Detective Williams said.

Josie held up her bandaged arm for them to see.

"Because Bugsy had almost taken my arm off and I was focused on making sure he didn't do the same thing to my face."

56

"Sure, that makes sense," Detective Swan said as she closed her notebook and slid it back into her pocket.

Then we all turned toward the door when we heard it click open and my mother trailed by Millie and Jill entered the suite laughing. When they spotted the cops, they stopped laughing but continued to sway back and forth on their feet.

"I didn't think we were doing the strippers until Saturday," my mother slurred.

"These are real cops, Mom," I said, shaking my head. "This is Detective Williams and Detective Swan."

"Nice to meet ya," my mother said, giving them a tipsy salute. "Hang on. What are the cops doing here?"

"Investigating a murder," I said without emotion.

"Really? Again? What did you do, darling?" she said, staring at me.

"I think we should order some coffee," I said, still shaking my head at my mother. "Have a seat, Mom."

"Good idea," Millie said as she collapsed into a chair.

"I think we'll be going," Detective Williams said, getting to his feet. He glanced around with a nondescript expression fixed on his face. Working for the Vegas police had obviously inured him to the realities of dealing with inebriated tourists. "Thanks for your time. You'll be here until Sunday. Is that correct?"

"It is," I said, getting up to shake hands with both of them.

"Cute dogs," Detective Swan said, reaching out to pet Squirrel. "Thanks for your help. If we have any other questions, we'll be in touch."

"We'll be around," I said, escorting them to the door. When they had left, I turned around and saw my mother passed out on one of the couches. I glanced at Millie and Jill who weren't far behind her. "Where did you guys go?"

"Just downstairs," Millie said, her eyes closed. "After we won all that money, we decided to celebrate with some shots."

"How much did you win?" I said, surprised.

"I won six grand," Millie said.

"I'm up about five," Jill said with a sleepy whisper. "I have no idea how much your mother won."

"But it was a lot," Millie said, drifting off to sleep.

My mother stirred, eventually came to, then sat up on the couch. It took her a few seconds to focus before she located me across the room.

"Hey, wait a sec," she slurred through a deep scowl. "Who's dead?"

"Sergei," I said.

"The guy at dinner?"

"Yeah."

"What happened to him?"

"We're not sure," I said.

"Okay," she said, yawning as she stretched back out on the couch. "Remember to tell me all about it in the morning."

58

"It's already morning, Mom."

"Then remember to tell me all about it in the afternoon."

Chapter 8

Thursday

By noon, I was nibbling on fruit and cheese and pounding ice water after spending the previous hour alternating between short bursts in the torrid sun and plunges into the pool to cool off. Each time I climbed out of the pool, I splashed water on the tile to ensure the bottom of my feet didn't blister during the short walk back to the cabana. Ninety was a hot summer day in Clay Bay, but here in the Vegas ninety was probably considered a cold snap at this time of year. I glanced up at the Hedaya sign on the outside of the building and couldn't miss the digital temperature display that read 108.

I grabbed a handful of grapes and shook my head at the two spaniels who were on the lookout for a snack.

"No grapes for you guys," I said, reaching into my bag and removing a plastic bag of dog treats. I tossed two each to both dogs. They snatched them out of mid-air and quickly chomped through them then settled back down under the mist. It was a hot day for them to be outside, but they seemed quite comfortable in the shade as the cool droplets floated down onto them.

I ate a couple of the grapes as I looked around the pool area and spotted Chef Claire strolling our way. I gave her a wave and soon she was stretched out next to me on the adjacent lounger.

60

"You made it," I said, lowering my sunglasses to get a good look at her. "What time did you get in last night?"

"Had to be after five," she said, slathering sunscreen over her arms and legs.

"Interesting," I said, grinning at her.

"No, it was nothing like that," Chef Claire said, shaking her head. "Louie and I were just catching up."

"So, no fireworks between you two?"

"No. We're just friends."

"Does Louie know that?" I said. "I couldn't miss some of the looks he was giving you."

"I'm sure he does," Chef Claire said, then paused to give it some thought. "At least, I think he does."

"Who does what?" Josie said, stirring from her nap.

"She's alive," I said, glancing over at her.

Josie yawned as she rubbed her eyes and slid her sunglasses on.

"I needed that," she said, then leaned forward to speak to Chef Claire. "How are you feeling?"

"I'm fine. I had my last glass of champagne around one. I guess we can't say the same for the three passed out in the living room."

"We tried to wake them up but finally decided to leave them there," I said, tossing another treat to each spaniel.

"Are they still out?" Josie said.

"Oh, yeah," Chef Claire said, chuckling. "I left them a note that we were down here. So, what's the plan for tonight?"

"We've got reservations at Craftsteak. Seven o'clock. And then Hedaya has comped us for the late show he's got running in his main auditorium," I said.

"What's the show?" Chef Claire said.

"It's some combination of acrobats and aerialists," I said. "It sounds like a Cirque de Soleil show, but Hedaya says it's different. And better."

"What do you expect him to say?" Josie said, laughing.

"Yeah, I know. Apparently, a couple that was at dinner last night are two of the featured performers," I said.

"So, it's a Russian show?" Chef Claire said.

"I think so," I said, glancing around the pool area that was beginning to fill up. "What do you guys want to do?"

"Sun, swim, sun, swim, snack, nap, shower, dinner, show," Josie recited without moving on the lounger. "I'll play it by ear from there."

"Nice to see you've been giving it some serious thought," I said, laughing.

"Hey, it's what I do," she said, sitting up briefly to lower her sunglasses and grin at us. "How are you gonna spend the day?"

"Probably a variation on your plan," I said, getting to my feet. "But I think we should get these guys back inside the air conditioning. It's too hot out here for them."

"You want some help?" Josie said.

62

"No, I'll take the dogs up to the suite and check on the Three Musketeers. I'll be right back."

"Write if you get work," Josie said, pulling her baseball cap further down.

I pulled a long tee shirt over my bathing suit and attached leads to both dogs. We headed for the side entrance of the casino. The automatic doors opened, and I felt the temperature drop by at least forty degrees. I shivered and took a few steps to one side just inside the entrance to give a group of people enough room to get past me and the dogs. I glanced down at the spaniels who had also come to a stop and sat down on their haunches. They stared up at me, waiting for instructions.

"You guys really are well-trained, aren't you?"

Both spaniels stood and wagged their tails. I rubbed their heads then began a slow stroll down a long hallway that led to a bank of elevators. On the way, I spied several yellow signs indicating a construction zone. Three strips of yellow tape stretched across the entrance to the vodka bar named Moscow Nights. Remembering Sergei's promise of a tour, I stopped directly in front of the bar and considered my options.

Given the fact that the owner was dead, I wondered if I could ask Hedaya to give me a tour of the bar and the technology behind its famous tasting room and ice bar. But knowing how busy he must be running a casino this size, it seemed like a major imposition to ask him to take time out of his day. I could certainly

63

handle it on my own, especially if I could manage to get a few minutes with one or more of the workers handling the renovations.

I stood outside for several moments with the dogs patiently sitting at my heels then I remembered the key Josie had removed from the enormous lizard. Then I remembered that Hedaya had chosen not to share that particular bit of news with the police. That either meant that Hedaya was part of something associated with the key, or he, like me, was also in the dark about its significance. Either way, I wondered if I might be able to shed some light on whether or not the key was an important piece of some sort of Russian plot. I spent a few more minutes dreaming up all sorts of possible schemes that might be happening inside the casino, or possibly the vodka bar I was standing directly in front of.

And even if it turned out that the key was merely what Sergei used to open his locker at the gym, I would still be using my time wisely by taking a tour of the bar and determining if there might be some ideas we could *borrow* and incorporate into our two restaurants. Knowing that I could use that as a plausible excuse for showing up uninvited, I glanced down at the dogs who continued to stare expectantly at the entrance.

"That's right," I said to them. "You guys must be in there all the time."

I glanced around at the people who streamed past me in both directions without giving me a second look. Then my Snoopmeter redlined. I nodded to myself, took one more look around, then led the dogs past the yellow tape and stepped inside the dimly lit establishment.

Chapter 9

I stood in the doorway and let my eyes adjust to the light. I knelt down and removed the leads from the dogs. They both picked up various scents and wagged their tails as they trotted off to begin exploring the familiar surroundings.

"Hello," I called out. "Anyone here?"

Receiving no response, I checked my watch and decided the work crew was possibly on their lunch break. Or, more likely, they had heard the news about Sergei's death and were taking the day off to mourn and regroup. I called out again, heard no response, then began exploring the main lounge. It was upscale with a lot of wood and brass and a wide variety of stained glass chandeliers and antique lamps that appeared to be authentic. Various photos of what I assumed were shots of the Russian landscape and places of interest in and around Moscow filled the walls. I walked to the main bar and noticed it was lit from underneath which highlighted the ice bar that had to be at least fifty feet long. I ran my hand over the smooth surface, and it reminded me of the ice you'd find at a curling rink. In fact, I decided, if concentric circles were painted on both ends of the bar, patrons could stand at either end and drink their vodka while sliding small metal pucks along the ice, similar to the ones used in the shuffleboard games often found in bars at home. I made a mental note to check with Chef Claire and Josie about how goofy of an idea it was. It wouldn't be the first time curling and drinking had shown up in the same sentence, and my idea eliminated the problem of dealing with forty-pound granite rocks and wearing yourself out pushing a broom over the ice trying to control them.

The area being renovated appeared to be further back, and I followed the dogs who were already surveying the scene and sniffing the floor covered with a thick layer of sawdust and drywall remnants. They paused to look up when they saw me approach then wagged their tails and went back to work. I walked up a set of steps to a smaller area that was even more well-appointed than the main lounge. This was evident even though drop cloths were draped over the tables and what I assumed were plush chairs and couches. I looked back at the main lounge and did a quick count. It appeared that the room could comfortably hold a couple of hundred people, and I assumed that the further back you wanted to sit, the more exclusive each area became. But it was the large, windowless area in the very back of the bar that caught and held my attention. A large stainless-steel door blocked access to what I was sure was the coveted tasting room.

"Hello," I called out again. "Anybody here?"

I shrugged when I received no response then headed for the door. It had a latch similar to the ones the freezers and walk-in coolers had at our restaurants. The door opened easily and I stepped inside to look around. I fumbled for the light switch and soon the room was bathed in light. Both dogs followed me inside and I pulled the door behind me but left it ajar. I glanced around

67

and noticed the rough condition of the partially renovated space. I was immediately concerned about the jagged pieces of wood and nails I saw on the floor. There were also a couple of sections that had been torn up which created recesses in the floor about a foot deep. I glanced at the dogs.

"Stay. Moose. Squirrel. Stay."

Both dogs heeled at my feet and glanced up at me waiting for further instructions.

"Good dogs," I said, nodding at them. Whatever nefarious activities Sergei may have been involved with, I had to give him props for the way he had trained his dogs.

"Stay," I repeated as I took a few steps forward to examine the ice bar inside the tasting room. It was smaller than the one in the main area, but it appeared to be identical in design. I glanced back at the dogs. "Stay."

Both dogs got the message and stretched out on the floor with their heads propped up on their front paws as they watched me closely. I scanned the windowless room and determined that it could hold around fifteen people. Behind the bar were dozens of different bottles I assumed were vodkas from all over the world. I recognized some of them, but many had labels written in Russian.

Even with the door partially open, it was obvious that the room was kept well below freezing. And in an obvious attempt to make patrons feel as comfortable as possible, as well as enhance the overall Russian experience, several mink coats and Cossack uniforms were hanging inside a small coat room near the bar.

I shivered and knew I wouldn't last long in this environment wearing only a tee shirt over my bathing suit. So, I grabbed my phone to call Chef Claire and tell her to meet me here since I was sure she would definitely get a kick out of the place. But I couldn't get any cell reception inside the thick-walled freezer and was just about to step outside to make the call when I heard voices. Torn between revealing myself and trying to explain my presence or simply waiting it out, I decided to stay put for the moment. I slid the phone back into my bag and leaned my head next to the crack in the door.

"Look, Natalie," an obviously annoyed man said. "I don't know what to tell you."

"Tell me what I want to know," she snapped.

I recognized the woman's voice and accent immediately. The spy I'd eaten dinner next to last night was obviously displeased with the man's response. I leaned forward until my ear was pressed against the edge of the metal door.

"If I knew where it was, I would tell you," the man said, his voice rising. "You know how Sergei was. He never told us anything other than do this, do that. Whatever his actual plans were, assuming he had any, you'd have to ask him."

"That's going to be a bit difficult to do now, wouldn't you say?" Natalie said.

Good point, I said to myself with a nod.

"Why don't you stop by in a couple of days when we get back to work?" the man said, obviously looking for a way to end the conversation. "Maybe Sergei mentioned something to one of the other workers."

"If he didn't tell you, I doubt if he told anyone else," she said, calming down a bit. "Maybe I'll swing by his house and talk with Maria."

"That sounds like a good idea," the man said.

"Okay," Natalie said. "But if I find out you've been lying to me, Mika, we're going to have a problem. Do we understand each other?"

I thought I heard the man gulp but could have been mistaken. I shivered again and ran my hands up and down my arms. I listened closely to the sound of receding footsteps and was about to poke my head out when the man spoke.

"What the heck?"

I heard him walking toward the tasting room, and my stomach dropped when I realized, like Lucy, I was about to have some serious explaining to do. I took a few steps back from the door and moved to one side. I glanced down at the dogs who had their heads cocked and were giving me a strange look.

"Stay," I whispered to the spaniels.

"I can't believe those idiots did it again," the man named Mika said.

"What?" Natalie said.

"They left the light on in the tasting room and the door open. How many times do I have to tell them not to do that?"

I stared at the small opening in the door, and a hand emerged, fumbled for the light switch, then the tasting room went dark. Then I heard the door slam shut. I stood in the dark for several seconds, then worked my way along the door and turned the lights back on. The dogs continued to stare up at me as I grabbed both their leads and attached them to their collars.

"You guys ready to get out of here?"

Both dogs hopped to their feet and I reached for the door handle and pulled. Then pushed. Then pulled again. My stomach dropped again as I frantically looked for a way to open the door. Then I leaned against the cold metal and shook my head in disbelief. I glanced down at the dogs, took a long look around the tasting room then slid to the floor with my back still pressed up against the locked door.

"Crap."

Chapter 10

It didn't take me long to recognize the plight the dogs and I were facing. Locked inside any sort of structure beyond one's will was enough to push the panic button. Being locked inside a freezer that no one else knew I was in was something else altogether. I continued to hug myself for warmth as I looked around the tasting bar that had been turned into a construction zone. I did my best to remain calm as I glanced around looking for any sign of a possible escape route. Then my eyes landed on what would prove to be very valuable items until I did.

I walked around the bar to the coat room and grabbed one of the fur coats. It was thick and heavy and I immediately began to feel warmer when I pulled it on. I was about to refocus on a possible means of escape when I spotted a long row of hats sitting above the collection of coats patrons wore while drinking their vodka and eating caviar. I grabbed one of the Cossack hats and put it on. It immediately dropped over my ears. I took a look at myself in the mirror behind the bar and shook my head as I glanced over at the spaniels who were both watching me closely.

"Sexy, huh?" I said, striking a pose for them.

Since I knew that people trapped in the cold lost most of their body heat through their head, I rummaged through the hats until I found the smallest one I could find and pulled it on. I buttoned the fur coat then scanned the bar area. Deciding that the dogs were

72

probably thirsty, I reached down into the sink below the bar and turned on the faucet. Nothing came out and I realized that the water had been turned off during the renovation. I scanned the inventory of bottles on glass shelves behind the bar, then spotted a small refrigerator that was emitting a small hum. Since power tools were obviously needed to complete the construction work, the electricity was still on. I headed for the fridge.

Inside, I spotted several bottles of water, both flat and fizzy. I grabbed a couple large bottles of an imported flat water we sold at both restaurants for about six bucks a bottle. I could only imagine what Sergei charged for it here. I glanced around and spied a large metal bowl, wiped it down, then poured both bottles into it. I set it on top of the ice bar while I searched for a spot on the floor to put it. The uneven floor, combined with the thick layer of sawdust and drywall dust, was a complete mess. In addition, the thought of the dogs walking through the sawdust that had to be an inch thick in spots seemed dangerous for them given the fact that nails, shards of metal, and other sharp objects might be lurking beneath the surface.

Stymied for the moment, I eventually spotted a broom and dragged it through the sawdust to create a small path for the dogs. I set the broom down then called them. They slowly trotted toward me and I removed their leads. I placed the large bowl of water down on the floor directly in front of me. They drank for a long time making a racket that had me laughing. While they quenched their thirst, I decided to join them. I grabbed a bottle of carbonated

Russian mineral water from the fridge and downed half of it. I paused to burp loudly. I took another long swallow then set the bottle down on the bar.

The problem of not dying from thirst solved, I turned back to the more pressing problem of not freezing to death. Since the man talking to Natalie had mentioned that the work crew wouldn't be back for a few days, I needed some sort of plan to keep our core temperatures as high as possible. I looked around the space wondering if it would be possible to build some sort of shelter in case we ended up having to spend the night. I considered heading for the far corner of the tasting room and using a couple of tables and the back wall as the basis for a temporary shelter. I figured I could use the Cossack coats to create a makeshift tent, then pile several other coats on the floor for bedding.

I was just about to begin my work when I saw something slithering across the room underneath the blanket of sawdust. A mouse, I hoped. But if it was, it was the biggest mouse I'd ever seen. Fearing it was a rat, I quickly discarded my plan and glanced around. Since the last thing I wanted to do was stretch out on a floor with vermin looking for a late-night cuddle, I scanned the tasting room again. The dogs and I would be able to get up off the floor by sliding some tables together, but I wasn't sure they'd provide enough stability for the dogs and me. And falling off the tables onto the floor in the middle of the night, should it come to that, wasn't an option.

Then I stared at the ice bar that stretched out in front of me. It was about twenty feet long and around four feet wide. And I realized that if I could figure out a way to keep the bone-chilling cold of the ice minimized, all three of us might be able to get comfortable and, more importantly, keep hypothermia at bay. I grabbed two of the Cossack coats and stacked them on top of each other on the bar. I stood back to take a look then added two more. Then I grabbed two of the furs and laid them on top of the other coats. I pressed my hands down on them and nodded. Deciding that the mattress was done, I grabbed two more of the furs to use as blankets along with a couple of Cossack hats for pillows and set them down on the bar next to the makeshift bed I'd just built.

I had no idea if we were going to be forced to use the bed I'd just made, but I wasn't taking any chances. Then I glanced down at the dogs who continued to be right there in the moment with me. Despite my increasing discomfort from the cold and the fact I might end up spending my bachelorette weekend locked inside a freezer, I beamed at the spaniels.

"You guys are pretty reliable, aren't you?"

I gave them a quick once-over and realized that they continued to stand in the thick blanket of sawdust that might be hiding all sorts of items that could hurt them. And if they caught sight of whatever rodent was lurking somewhere beneath the layer of wood shavings, they might dash off in pursuit and end up doing some serious damage to themselves.

I patted the aluminum counter next to the sink underneath the bar, and both spaniels approached and stared up at me. I tapped the counter again, and Moose hopped up onto the counter then onto the bar. He did a few lazy circles then stretched out on top of the makeshift mattress and almost disappeared from sight under the minks. Squirrel followed suit, and soon both dogs were lying next to each other and watching to see what my next move was.

Feeling a hunger pang, I glanced around for something to eat. The only thing in sight were several tins of Russian caviar. I grimaced and shook my head in disgust. About the only thing worse than eating fish would have to be eating the eggs fish come from. I say would have to be because none of the vile *delicacy* had ever passed my lips.

But my hunger worsened, and I picked up one of the small round tins and unsuccessfully tried to read the label that was written in Russian. I shook the can, turned it upside down then shook it again. My stomach rumbled again, and I began to wonder if perhaps the taste and texture of caviar might surprise me.

Perhaps it's categorization as a delicacy was well-deserved and I'd been missing out all these years.

Perhaps it was, in fact, a delicious treat I would come to crave on a regular basis.

Perhaps it tasted like another food I enjoyed, and all I needed to do was close my eyes while I ate it and thought about something else.

Perhaps chicken.

Perhaps.

I stared suspiciously at the can I was holding. My hunger wasn't going anywhere and would only be deepening over the coming hours. Trying to put aside thoughts about my dinner plans for a juicy New York strip with salad and the mushroom medley served on a sizzling metal platter Craftsteak was famous for, I popped the lid on the can of caviar and tentatively dipped my pinkie. I examined the small pile of black fish eggs on the end of my finger then slowly raised my hand and slid it into my mouth.

Then I gagged and spit fish eggs across the floor. They sunk beneath the surface of the sawdust and disappeared from sight. Unfortunately, it wasn't as easy getting the taste out of my mouth. I grabbed the bottle of fizzy water and chugged. Then I hacked, spit again and took another long pull from the bottle. The dogs sat up and stared at me with their heads cocked and remained that way until I reached out to pet them. They settled back onto the furs and huddled close to each other.

I put the lid back on the can of caviar and stared at it in disbelief. Delicacy indeed.

Russian caviar wasn't the worst thing I'd ever tasted.

But it was a lot like it.

I climbed up on the bar onto the makeshift mattress and was cocooned from the cold as the thick fur enveloped me. Regardless of how long we might end up inside the tasting bar from hell, I knew that, if we did somehow manage to not make it out alive, the official cause of death wouldn't be listed as hypothermia. I stretched out until I was comfortable then pulled one of the remaining furs up under my chin. Both dogs waited until I was settled in underneath the mink blanket then got up and stretched out directly in front of me. I draped an arm over both of them, adjusted the hat I was still wearing and used another of the Cossack hats as a pillow.

"Sorry to get you guys into this mess."

I felt the gentle thump of both dogs' tails against the coats.

"This is something else, huh?" I closed my eyes in an attempt to relax and not think about the plight we were in. Then I felt a familiar twinge and I opened my eyes and shook my head.

"Crap. I need to pee."

Both dogs perked up and looked at me expectantly. Then they both stood on top of the bar and glanced around.

"You guys need to pee?"

Both dogs headed to the edge of the bar and began pacing back and forth. I sat up and looked around the bar then shrugged at them.

"I'm afraid we're going to have to break our cardinal rule about peeing inside, huh?" I said to them, then caught myself. "I mean, you guys are. I'm going to try to hold it. But you go ahead, just this one time. Go pee."

The spaniels seemed to understand exactly what I was saying and hopped down onto the sink then the sawdust-covered floor. Moose led the way, and they tentatively headed for the back corner of the freezer to take care of business. A few minutes later,

78

they were back up on the bar next to me, stretched out and looking a lot more comfortable.

"You guys are really smart," I said, petting both of them.

Moose tried to inch closer to me, and I put a hand out to keep him off my bladder. I wiggled back a few inches and gently thumped his side.

"No, you won't be able to sit there," I said, doing my best to ignore the pressure that was building up.

I closed my eyes and ran through a variety of options, all of them fruitless, about how to get out of the freezer. Deciding that we would need to be rescued, I finally quit thinking and officially began to wait. Waiting for someone to realize I was gone and come looking.

But I didn't like the chances that anyone would put two and two together and come looking for us in here. Trapped inside a deep freeze posing as upscale entertainment, surrounded by bottles of vodka and tins of disgusting Russian caviar. By the time I finally got my attention off my full bladder, the dogs were snoring gently. Since I was operating on three hours of sleep, I decided to join them. I tucked the fur blanket under my chin, used two of the Cossack hats to create a surprisingly comfortable pillow, and drifted off to sleep on top of the ice bar.

I dreamt hard.

I don't remember all my dreams, but one did resonate. I was standing at the edge of the tasting room bar, knee deep in sawdust, sliding miniature Komodo Dragons down the ice toward a series of concentric circles that were all yellow. I was winning my curling match with Sergei who was giving me a dead-eyed stare from the other end of the bar. He was having a hard time playing the game since his right arm was bent at an odd angle. Sergei wiped the foam away from his mouth with his good hand then slid one of the metal lizards down the bar while trying to fight off Josie who was doing her best to perform emergency surgery on him.

"What's the key for, Sergei?" I called out every time one of the lizards slid along the ice.

But he ignored me and kept trying to swat Josie away with his good hand. Then I felt a hand nudging my shoulder to get my attention. I glanced over and saw the bartender holding out a shot of clear liquid. I accepted the shot glass and tossed back a frigid mouthful of vodka. I set the glass down and glanced at the bartender to thank him.

Frank Zappa was behind the bar drying a glass with a towel and staring back at me with a big grin. He nodded when I voiced my thanks, but instead of saying you're welcome, he broke into song.

"Watch out where the Huskies go, and don't you eat that yellow snow."

"Thanks, Frank. Good advice," I said, nodding. "And I should also stay away from damp patches of sawdust, right?"

Frank shrugged.

"It probably couldn't be any worse than the caviar."

"It's hard to argue with your logic, Frank."

80

Chapter 11

I woke to the sound of metal on metal and low, guttural growls from both spaniels. It took me a few seconds, but when I realized the tasting room door was opening, I tried to sit up. But I remained immobilized, attached to the bar. Wondering if I was still dreaming, I glanced around the best I could for signs of Frank but could only make out the blurred images of various people walking toward me. I blinked several times and again tried to lift my head off the bar, but soon realized the side of my face was definitely stuck and I wasn't going anywhere.

"Darling, are you all right?"

"Hi, Mom. Yeah, I'm sure I'll be fine," I said, not moving.

"Well, you don't look very happy to see us," my mother said, reaching out to pet both dogs who were standing on the bar wagging their tails.

"I think I'm stuck," I said.

"Stuck?" Hedaya said as he came to a stop next to my mother.

"Hi, Hedaya," I said. "Yeah, my head must have slipped off the hat I was using for a pillow. My face is stuck to the bar."

"Unbelievable," Josie said, shaking her head. "Should I even ask?"

"Probably not," I said. "You know how at least one kid every winter would try to lick a frostbitten pole and get their tongue stuck?"

81

"Yes, darling," my mother said, still staring in disbelief at me. "How could I forget? Especially since one of them was you."

"We need some hot water," Hedaya said, glancing around the tasting room.

"I think the water is off during the renovation," I said, managing to blink several times.

"Let me call someone," Hedaya said, reaching for his phone.

"You won't get any reception in here," I said, then grimaced when I felt my bladder wake up.

"Then hang on," he said, heading for the door. "I'll be right back."

"Wait a sec, Hedaya," Josie said, approaching the bar. "This will work."

I stared at the large cup she was holding.

"What's that?" I said, doing my best to make eye contact.

"Coffee."

"You're going to pour hot coffee on me?" I said.

"Actually, I'm going to pour it on the bar," she said, then paused. "Unless you'd like to stay there and wait."

"No, okay," I said, squeezing my thighs together as my bladder made its presence known. "Just be careful."

"Says the woman with her face stuck to an ice bar," Josie said, shaking her head. "Just try not to move."

"Funny."

82

Josie poured a small amount of coffee next to my face, and the smell overwhelmed me. I tried to move my head but was still stuck fast.

"Hang on," Josie said, moving my hair back as best she could and carefully pouring some more of the hot beverage close to my face.

I felt some of the skin come free.

"How's that?" Josie said.

"I think it's working."

"Good. Cream, no sugar. Just the way you like it."

"I'm really not in the mood," I snapped, then spotted my mother holding up her phone. "Mom, what are you doing?"

"Just capturing the moment for posterity," she said as she snapped several pictures.

"Hold still," Josie said, gently pouring more coffee onto the bar.

I felt the coffee as it worked its way between my face and the ice and part of my cheek popped free.

"One more time," I said, nodding at Josie.

She poured again and I felt air between my face and the bar. I slowly lifted my head, encountered no resistance, then sat up. I gently touched the side of my face and caught a glimpse of myself in the mirror behind the bar. The Cossack hat was tilted at a weird angle, and the tee shirt I was wearing over my bathing suit had slipped off my shoulders. My hair was matted and now wet in places from the coffee, and I had the fur coat I'd used as a blanket

83

draped over my arms. But it was the large pink patch of freezer-burned skin covering one side of my face that had me most concerned.

"I'm ready for my closeup, Mr. DeMille," I said, shaking my head.

"Let's get you out of here," Hedaya said as he gently helped me step down to the edge of the sink then onto the floor. "You must be freezing."

"Actually, I need to pee," I said, bouncing up and down on my toes.

"The bathrooms are inside the main bar. Just off to the right."

"C'mon, Nanuck," Josie said, leading me by the arm. "Let's get you cleaned up."

Josie carefully led the way through the sawdust, and we exited the tasting room. The air conditioning was on full blast, and I continued to hold the mink coat draped over my shoulders.

"What time is it?" I said.

"It's just after five," Josie said, holding the bathroom door open for me.

"Five? Morning or afternoon?"

"Afternoon," she said, hopping up to sit on the counter as I raced for one of the stalls. "You've been gone about four hours. After we realized you were gone, we started looking for you. Eventually, we wondered if you might have stopped by the bar. And I must say that, once again, you somehow managed to surprise and delight."

"Shut it."

I flushed the toilet and headed for the row of sinks. I turned on one of the taps and was grateful to find that the water in the main bar was working. I washed my hands then splashed several handfuls of hot water on my face, grimacing every time the water touched the frozen side of my face. I accepted the hairbrush Josie was holding out. I worked on myself for a few minutes until I realized it was the best I could do until I got back to the suite and took a hot shower and washed my hair.

"You want to tell me what happened?" Josie said, raising an eyebrow at me.

"Let's wait until everyone gets back to the suite," I said, gently touching the freezer burn on the side of my face.

"Because this is a story you're only going to be telling once, right?" Josie said, laughing.

"Nothing gets past you," I said, patting my face dry with paper towels. "Are you ready to go?"

"Lead the way," she said, hopping off the counter and following me toward the door.

I stepped inside the main lounge and saw my mother and Hedaya waiting with the dogs.

"Where's everyone else?" I said to my mother.

"They've been on the hunt for you as well," she said. "But we just called them. We're all going to meet back at the suite. Everyone is dying to hear this one."

"I need to shower first," I said, walking out of the bar and heading straight for the elevators.

"I'm sure it will be worth the wait," my mother said, grinning at Hedaya.

"Do you need to see a doctor?" Hedaya said, studying my face.

"No, I don't think so," I said. "It's already starting to feel a bit better."

"Well, just let me know if you change your mind," he said, pressing the up button.

One of the elevators arrived, and Hedaya held the door open then stepped inside and stood between Moose and Squirrel. He leaned down to pet both of them then caught the look my mother was giving him.

"What is it?"

"You're coming with us?" my mother said, surprised.

"Are you kidding? I gotta hear this," he said with a grin.

"Are you sure you're okay?" Josie said as the elevator rose.

"Yeah, I'm fine," I said, nodding. "But I need to brush my teeth."

"Okay," she said, giving me a puzzled look. "Probably wouldn't be my first choice, but whatever floats your boat."

"I ate caviar," I said, scowling. "Disgusting."

I leaned back against the elevator wall and started humming. A few seconds later, Josie glanced over at me.

"What's that song you're humming?"

86

"Frank Zappa."

Chapter 12

I began telling my tale of woe and took advantage of the stunned silence I was receiving by toweling off my hair. I draped the towel over my shoulder then sipped hot tea and glanced around waiting for the first of what I assumed would be several questions.

"So," Millie said, frowning. "You got locked inside the ice bar and fell asleep?"

"Yes," I said, nodding as I took another sip. "Actually, it was the tasting room in the back of the bar."

"Got it," Millie said, shaking her head.

"And you got your face stuck to the top of the bar?" Jill said.

"To the ice, yes," I said, setting my cup down on the table in front of me. "And then Josie poured coffee on it." I gently touched the side of my face. "How does it look?"

"Kinda like you fell on a waffle iron," Josie said, then expounded. "Assuming you were making waffles with a teeny-tiny pattern."

"Thanks for clarifying," I said, making a face at her.

"Does it hurt?" Millie said, leaning closer to get a better look.

"Not really," I said. "It's sort of like the tingle you get in your toes when you're outside in winter."

"What on earth were you doing in there, darling?"

"I was on my way up to the suite to check on you guys and get the dogs out of the heat," I said, rubbing lotion on my face.

88

"Then I walked past Moscow Nights and thought I'd check out the ice bar."

My mother listened closely then nodded and motioned for me to continue.

"And when I went inside, I realized that no one was working."

"They've shut the construction down for a few days given what happened to Sergei," Hedaya said.

"That makes sense," I said. "After I went inside, I just started wandering around. I spotted the freezer door, realized it was the entrance to the tasting room and walked inside. Before I knew it, I heard Natalie and some guy named Mika talking. So, rather than get busted for snooping, I decided to wait it out until they left." I looked at Hedaya. "It sounded like Mika is the head of the crew handling the renovations."

"He is," Hedaya said. "What were they talking about?"

"I couldn't be sure," I said. "But it sounded like they were discussing some sort of situation with Sergei. It could have been something to do with the key Bugsy swallowed, right?"

"I suppose that's a logical assumption," he said.

"By the way, how is he doing?" I said, glancing back and forth between Hedaya and Josie.

"He's fine," Hedaya said, smiling at Josie. "And he should be ready for solid food tomorrow."

"Just not too solid, right?" Josie said. "Try to keep him away from the scrap metal for a while."

89

"I'll do that," he said, laughing. Then he turned back to me. "Did they mention anything specific?"

"Not while I was listening to them. But they were both annoyed at different times. What significance do you attach to that key? Something like a safe filled with money?"

"I doubt it," Hedaya said, shaking his head. "Given the people who might be involved, money is the least of their worries."

"Then it has to be information, right?" I said, my neurons beginning to fire.

"That, too, is a logical assumption to make," Hedaya said, staring off at the wall.

"Do you know which person the information might pertain to?"

"It could be any of them," he said with a shrug. "I'm sure everyone in that group of Russians has things in their past they wouldn't want shared."

"Do you know what sort of information it might be?"

"I could make several guesses," he said, again shrugging. "And all of them quite speculative at this point."

"Have you told the police about the key yet?" I whispered, leaning in close to him.

"No. And I don't plan to do that."

"Because the information might be something about you?" I said, studying him closely.

90

"One never knows," he said in a cryptic tone that only increased my level of curiosity.

"Please, darling," my mother said, shaking her head at my incessant questions. "Don't annoy Hedaya."

"No, it's quite all right," he said, glancing at my mother. "I don't mind. Actually, I was wondering if Suzy might be able to help me out."

"You were?" my mother and I said in unison.

"Yes," Hedaya said, turning to me. "Since I don't want to bring the police into this, I might be able to use your expertise. Your mother speaks very highly of your powers of deduction."

"She does?"

"I wouldn't read too much into that, Hedaya. I tend to babble when I drink," my mother said. "Darling, we are here to celebrate your upcoming nuptials. Why on earth would you want to get involved in something like this?"

I gave my mother a blank stare.

"Forget I even asked," she said, shaking her head. "Just promise me a few things."

"Sure, Mom," I said, leaning forward. "What's on your mind?"

"First, you can't let it interfere with our plans for the weekend. We've gone to great lengths to make this a memorable trip."

"Absolutely," I said, nodding. "I wouldn't do anything to ruin it, Mom."

"Good. Try to remember that. Second, you have to agree to confine your snooping to just asking some general questions and report back to Hedaya. Don't forget that these folks have just lost a good friend."

"Well, I don't think we can make that judgment yet, Mom. Sergei might have only been an acquaintance to a lot of them."

"You know what I mean, darling. Just try not to annoy the crap out of everybody, okay?"

"Of course," I said, my mind already racing. "I'm not a total idiot."

"I guess time will tell," she said, getting to her feet. "Okay, we need to get ready for dinner. And then we have tickets for the show after that. You can start your snooping in the morning while the rest of us are either gambling or hanging out at the pool. Got it?"

"Yeah, I got it, Mom," I said, chastised.

She got up and headed for the adjoining suite. I waited until I heard the door close then turned to Hedaya.

"Where are you going to be later on after the show is over?"

"I'll be around," Hedaya said, then nodded at my mother's bedroom. "But didn't she just tell you to wait until the morning to get started?"

"Oh, that," I said, waving it off. "Don't worry about it. It's this little game we play. She tells me not to do something, and I come up with a creative way to work around it. When she finally

92

figures out what I'm up to, she freaks out and yells at me. It gives her something to be mad about. It's sort of a win-win."

"A win-win?" Hedaya said, frowning.

"Yeah, I get to do some snooping and hopefully get some questions answered, and she gets to vent about what a horrible daughter I can be. It keeps her young."

"It must be working," Hedaya said, shrugging. "She looks fantastic."

"Yeah, I usually give her a lot to work with."

Chapter 13

For those of you who haven't had the pleasure of dining there, Craftsteak is an upscale steakhouse inside the MGM and well-known for the quality of its food. In addition to their steaks and sides, they offer a mushroom-medley served on a sizzling platter that is a total knee-buckler. Not surprisingly, we ended up ordering four orders to split between the six of us. Craftsteak is also known as a good place for celebrity sightings since many of the performing artists playing in town, and other visiting luminaries often eat in the restaurant.

So, it was without a lot of forethought that Chef Claire and I engaged in an impromptu game of *You know who that looks like?* right after our steaks arrived.

"No, it's not her," I said, shaking my head as I savored my first bite of steak. "She's taller than that."

"She's sitting down, Suzy," Chef Claire protested. "How the heck can you tell how tall she is?"

"Maybe you're right," I said, taking a sip of wine as I glanced around the restaurant. "Oh, my," I whispered like an awestruck teenager. "Isn't that…?"

"It certainly is," Chef Claire whispered back. "He's shorter than he looks on screen. Is that his wife with him?"

"Judging from all the people taking photos, he better hope so," I said, laughing.

94

Chef Claire laughed along and was about to reach for a mushroom when she stopped and frowned.

"What the heck?" she said, glancing at me. Then we both glared at Josie who stared back at us as she chewed a mouthful of food. "We turn our back for a second and this is what we get?"

"I have no idea what you're talking about," Josie finally managed after she swallowed. "But I guess the question is, did you come here to eat or hunt celebrities?"

I stared down at the two empty platters sitting between the three of us and shot Josie a final dirty look before asking our waiter for two more orders. I then hunkered down over my steak and baked potato like a prisoner guarding his food at mealtime.

After dinner, we thought about making the short walk back to Hedaya's place, but the temperature was still hovering in the nineties. We piled into a limo then headed directly to the auditorium where Kremlin Heights, an aerial show comprised of Russian performers, entertained us for the next hour and a half. At least they were all Russian according to the show's program. But ten minutes into the show, I knew that some liberties had been taken with at least one of the performers' background.

She was a woman by the name of Wanda who had been a member of a circus that had recently visited Clay Bay. It was a long and somewhat tortured story. Wanda and her brother had been the feature act in the *world famous* Pontilly Family Circus. But the brother-sister team had plans to leave the circus and move to Vegas to get off the road. Unfortunately, before they could do that, Mr. Pontilly, the old man who owned the circus, was killed and Wanda's brother had been arrested for his murder. He was now facing a lengthy prison sentence while Wanda was spending most of her time doing aerial somersaults for thousands of tourists willing to plunk down a hundred bucks just for the privilege of watching.

I nudged Josie with an elbow and nodded up at the woman who had just completed a triple somersault and been caught by a male aerialist hanging upside down on a trapeze about fifty feet above the stage.

"What?" Josie said, glancing over.

"Guess who?" I said, pointing at Wanda.

"Another round of Spot the Celebrity? Okay, I'll play," Josie said as she stared up at the woman I was focused on. "Let me guess. Meryl Streep has run off and joined the circus."

"Funny. Take a close look at her."

"Well, what do you know?" she said eventually. "I thought Wanda was joining Cirque de Soleil."

"She was," I said, shrugging. "In fact, I'm pretty sure she did."

"Maybe she got a better offer," Josie said. "She is good."

"But she's not Russian," I said, flipping through the program. "Man, you can't believe anything you read these days."

"Does it matter?" Josie said, staring up at multiple aerialists who were all flying through the air at the same time.

96

"No, I'm just making a point," I said. "I think I might stop by after the show." I caught the raised eyebrow she was giving me and shrugged. "You know, just to say hi."

"And pump her for some information about her fellow performers, right?"

"You're on fire tonight," I said, grinning. "You want to join me?"

"Normally, I'd love to tag along and watch you annoy a whole bunch of new people. But I promised your mom I'd play at least an hour of craps with her."

"Okay, then I'll look for you in the casino later on," I said, again focusing on the show.

"Just promise me you won't do anything stupid," she said, glancing over.

"You know I can't do that," I deadpanned without making eye contact. Then I flinched when she punched me on the shoulder. "Ow. Knock it off."

"I'm serious," Josie said. "This is supposed to be your bachelorette party. The plan is to have some fun."

"Oh, don't worry," I said, nodding vigorously with my lips pursed. "I'm sure I'll have lots of fun."

After the show, I headed backstage, dropped Hedaya's name to get past security, then found Wanda toweling off in one of the dressing rooms chatting with several other performers. When she spotted me, she shrieked and gave me a warm embrace.

"Suzy, it's so good to see you," she said, holding me by the shoulders as she took a good look. "Girls weekend, right?"

"It is," I said. "They're all down in the casino, but I thought I'd stop by to say hi. Great show."

"Thanks," she said, then downed half a bottle of water. She was about to say something else when she spotted the mark on my face. "What happened to you?"

"Oh, that," I said, shrugging. "Just a little freezer burn."

"Okay," she said, staring at me like I'd lost my mind.

"I thought you were working with Cirque."

"I was," Wanda said, shrugging. "But they were making noises about me joining one of their touring shows, and I'm just not ready to get back on the road. So, here I am."

"As a distant cousin of Nicolas the First, right?" I said, laughing.

"Hey, what can I tell you?" she said, laughing along. "I come from noble stock."

"How's your brother doing?"

"Oh, well, you know," she said, her mood darkening. "Miggy's lawyer is still trying to negotiate it down to manslaughter. So, we'll see."

"Well, I hope he's doing okay," I said. "Give him my best the next time you see him."

"I'll do that," Wanda said, forcing a smile. "So, what other plans do you guys have while you're in town?"

98

"Pretty much the usual," I said with a shrug. "And they haven't shared some of them with me yet. You know, they want me to be surprised."

"Sure, you gotta keep the bride-to-be on her toes," she said. "Look, several folks from the show are going clubbing tonight. You're welcome to join us."

"I would," I said, deciding it was time to toss my line in the water. "But I'm kinda working at the moment."

"Working?" she said, confused. "Doing what?"

"I'm helping Hedaya out with a problem he might have," I said, unable to come up with a better description.

"What sort of problem could Hedaya have?" she said, frowning. "The guy leads a very charmed life."

"Yes, he certainly does," I said, nodding. "But somebody killed the guy who owned the Russian vodka bar in Hedaya's rainforest last night."

"Do you have any idea how weird that sounds?" Wanda said.

"Yeah, I do. Hedaya was giving us a tour of his rooftop and was about to introduce us to Bugsy when we found Sergei's body inside the lizard's enclosure."

"So, the rumors about Hedaya having a thirteen-foot Komodo Dragon are true?" she said, raising an eyebrow.

"Oh, yeah," I said. "He's something else."

"It's so sad," Wanda said, shaking her head. "Everybody loved Sergei."

"Well, maybe not everybody," I said, frowning.

"Yeah, you do have a point," she said. "But he was a nice guy. We often head to Moscow Nights after a show. That tasting room in the back is something else."

"Yeah, it's a real hoot," I said, rubbing the side of my face. "Can I ask you a question?"

"Here we go," Wanda said, giving me a big grin.

"Yeah, I know," I said, shrugging. "Sorry."

"Go right ahead."

"I was just wondering who the two bleached blonde performers are," I said, nodding at the couple who were still wearing their leotards and snuggling in the corner of the dressing room. "They were at dinner last night, but I didn't get a chance to talk to them."

"Olga and Kosiny," Wanda said, glancing over.

"Are they really Russian?"

"Oh, yeah," she said. "The show isn't lying about that."

"The program said they're brother and sister," I said, grimacing as the couple came together for a long, deep kiss.

"No, that's a lie," Wanda said. "They aren't related."

"That's good," I said, sneaking another peek in their direction. "Because that would be really weird."

Wanda laughed.

"They started dating recently and rarely come up for air if you get my drift," she said.

"Yeah, I got it."

"Actually, Olga used to date Sergei," Wanda said. "She was doing everything she could to get her hooks into him, but he wasn't willing to settle down."

"I heard he was a committed bachelor," I said.

"I guess that's one way to describe it," Wanda said, frowning.

"Sergei was a player?"

"A total player. Olga fell hard for him and was pretty upset when he dumped her in no uncertain terms. Fortunately, Kosiny was there to catch her."

"In more ways than one, right?" I said.

"There you go," she said, then cocked her head when an idea emerged. "Actually, those two are going clubbing with us tonight. It might be a good chance to do a bit of...what do you call it?"

"Investigative work?"

"No, that's not it," she said, shaking her head.

"Snooping?" I whispered.

"That's the one," she said. "If you want to come along, we're going start at Club X upstairs. It plays mostly techno, so be prepared. It's loud. Just tell the guy working the door that you're with the Kremlin Heights group. Or I suppose since you're doing some work for him, you could just drop Hedaya's name."

"Maybe I'll do that," I said, glancing at the bleached blonde couple again. "Is there anything I should know about those two?"

"Not really," Wanda said. "Kosiny is your basic dumb jock. You know, nice house, nobody home. But Olga is really smart,

And she's a major flirt which drives Kosiny crazy. And he's got a temper he isn't shy about showing off."

"Do you think he's capable of hurting somebody?" I whispered.

"You mean, do I think he's capable of murder?" she whispered back.

"Yeah."

"That sounds like a major stretch," she said, shaking her head. "Unless he was trying to send Sergei a message and got carried away. How did he die? Nobody is revealing many details so far."

"The working theory so far is that he was poisoned," I said. "But a couple of body parts were bent at weird angles."

"Yuk," Wanda said with a deep frown.

"And whoever put Sergei inside the lizard enclosure had to get him over a ten-foot wall," I said.

"Well, if there's anybody who'd be strong enough to do that, it would be Kosiny."

"He is built like a linebacker," I said, nodding.

"Maybe that's his problem," Wanda said, laughing as she glanced over at the couple who were about to need the hose turned on them. "Played too many games without a helmet." Then she beamed at me and gave me another hug. "It's so good to see you. And you should think about coming with us tonight. It'll be fun."

"I'll see what I can do," I said, returning the embrace.

102

"I need to grab a shower then change," she said, reaching for her bag. "We should be upstairs at the club by midnight. Hope you can make it."

"Well, I'm not much of a clubber," I said, sneaking one final look at the blonde aerialists. "But I guess it couldn't hurt."

"When in Rome, right?"

"It's not Rome I'm worried about," I said, laughing.

"Don't worry," Wanda said, draping her bag over her shoulder. "What happens here, stays here."

"You don't really believe that, do you?"

"Of course not," she said, giving me an over the shoulder finger wave as she headed off. "But it seems to help the tourists relax."

Chapter 14

I found Hedaya in his office after making my way through three layers of security. By the time I made it past the final two security guards outside his office door wearing identical suits and matching earpieces, I was beginning to wonder if Hedaya was always this cautious or if Sergei's murder had caused him to increase the number of people assigned to keep him safe and sound. I stepped inside the massive office that was located down a hallway behind the registration desk on the first floor. He immediately got up from behind his desk and gestured at a sitting area. I sat down in a comfortable chair that seemed to be giving me a permanent hug. Hedaya sat down across from me and draped a leg over his knee.

"Would you like something to drink?" he said. "Perhaps a glass of champagne?"

"No, I'm good, thanks," I said, glancing around the office at dozens of photographs of Hedaya posing with famous politicians, athletes, and entertainers. "Do you know all these people or did you just have your photo taken with them?"

He glanced around the walls then casually shrugged.

"I know most of them quite well," he said.

"Including him?" I said, nodding at one of the photos.

104

"Oh, yes," Hedaya said, smiling at some memory. "He came to me for advice about how he might be able to turn around some of the problems he was having with his casinos on the East Coast."

"And?" I said, raising an eyebrow.

"He didn't listen," Hedaya said, laughing. "About a year later, he filed for bankruptcy."

"How hard is it to lose money running casinos?"

"I would imagine it's quite difficult," he said, shrugging. "But I really wouldn't know."

"Because you never lose money, right?"

"Consider it one of my basic *policies*," he said, laughing again as he raised his glass in toast. "So, how was the show?"

"It was great," I said. "And thanks so much for the tickets."

"You're very welcome," he said, setting his glass down. "Where's the rest of your entourage?"

"They're playing craps."

"Yes," he said, frowning. "Why am I not surprised?"

"What's wrong?"

"Your mother always kills me when she's here," he said, shaking his head. "I have no idea how she does it, but she usually takes at least a hundred grand from me."

"She probably cheats," I said, laughing.

"If she does, we certainly haven't been able to figure out how she's doing it," he said, sounding serious.

"What sort of help do you think you might need from me, Hedaya?"

"Yes," he said, nodding. "We need to talk about that." Hedaya stood up and began pacing slowly back and forth behind his chair. "I can't go into a lot of the details. But I can tell you that I've been worried about some…emerging Russian influence here in Vegas."

"Okay," I said, frowning. "You're worried that somebody might be trying to take over your casino?"

"Oh, my. Absolutely not. While I'm willing to tolerate their presence here since they're known to drop a ton of money, any attempt to try to muscle their way into my operations would be met with swift and direct action."

"By your security team, right?" I said, changing my mind about the champagne. "Maybe I will have a little splash."

Hedaya poured and handed me the glass.

"Partially," he said. "I have an excellent security team. But most of the response to any sort of overt Russian intrusion would be dealt with by people who have…let's call it, some serious juice."

"You're talking about the Feds."

Hedaya nodded.

"FBI?"

"Certainly. Among others."

"CIA?"

"Yes," he said, nodding.

"What on earth is the CIA doing in Vegas?" I said, surprised by that bit of news.

106

"Protecting the Homeland," he said with a grin. "What else?"

"Got it."

"And I imagine they also spend a lot of time protecting their assets," he said, then sat back to take a sip of champagne. He let his comment hang in the air as he studied my expression closely.

"Their assets?" I said, letting his comment and the possible implications wash over me. Then the lightbulb flickered. "Sergei was CIA?"

"Well done," Hedaya said, nodding at me. "Your reputation is well deserved. I was never able to officially confirm it, but it's definitely a possibility."

"But he was also working for the Russians, wasn't he?"

"Outstanding," he said, raising his glass in salute. "Again, that was never confirmed. But his ties to the Motherland were quite strong."

"Okay," I said, taking a small sip. "I guess it makes sense why you wouldn't want to bring the Vegas cops into this."

"No, I simply couldn't do that," Hedaya said. "While they are very good at what they do, they don't have the *finesse* required to handle a situation like the one I might be facing."

"And I do?" I said, frowning.

"Well, I guess we're going to find that out, aren't we?" he said, staring at me.

"I still don't know why you would ask me to help you out, Hedaya. You don't even know me."

"Actually, I've had conversations with some friends the past few months about you, Suzy," he said, picking at an imaginary piece of lint on his pants.

"What?" I said, stunned. "Who have you been talking to?"

"Well, Summerman was the first person who mentioned your name," Hedaya said without emotion. "He speaks very highly of you. He says you are the perfect blend of inquisitiveness, intelligence, and tenacity."

"Is that a nice way of saying I'm a nosy snoop who won't take no for an answer?"

"Tomato, tomahto."

"Sure, sure," I said, then leaned forward and lowered my voice. "How well do you know Summerman?"

"You mean, do I know about him being a part-timer?"

"You know?" I said, stunned again.

"Yes, I'm one of the few who does," Hedaya said. "And when Summerman told me how you pieced that together, I was very impressed."

"It really wasn't that hard," I said, shrugging it off.

"You're too modest. And you've obviously proven yourself to be someone who can keep a secret," Hedaya said, topping off our glasses.

"Well, if I started walking around talking about a guy who only spent three months a year as a living person, I'd be locked up and classified as a total wingnut."

Hedaya laughed and beamed at me.

108

"Indeed."

"Who else have you been talking to?"

"Doc and Merlin."

"Really?" I said, remembering my few interactions with the two men who worked with Summerman on various things I was clueless about. "I like Doc. But Merlin is a total pain in the butt."

"You'll get no argument from me," Hedaya said. "But Merlin's a genius. And geniuses have to be cut a wide path. Normally, I would be using their services, but they are currently working on something else for me."

"Here in Vegas?"

"No. In China," Hedaya said.

"Can you tell me what they're doing over there?" I said, studying him closely.

"No, I'm afraid that won't be possible," he said, shaking his head. "But it doesn't matter. It's not relevant."

"What exactly is the situation?" I said, leaning forward.

"It deals with the key."

"The one that Josie removed from Bugsy?"

"That's the one," he said. "And I can't thank her enough for what she did. He seems to be almost back to full strength."

"She's very good at what she does," I said, nodding.

"As are you," Hedaya said, again raising his glass to me.

"You want me to track down the significance of the key and figure out what it opens," I said.

109

"Yes. And, if possible, bring whatever is in the repository back to me," he said, nodding.

"What do you think it is?"

"I have no idea. But my hope is that the information deals with Alexi," Hedaya said.

"Your hope?" I said, frowning. "The guy at dinner? The oligarch who controls all the Russian oil?"

"That's him."

I sat quietly for a long time and waited for my thoughts to coalesce. Then I sat back in my chair and stared up at the ceiling before finally making eye contact.

"You've been wondering if Alexi might be working on our side of the street, right?"

"Keep going," Hedaya said, nodding as a small smile began to emerge.

"The FBI and CIA were under the impression that they had turned him," I said, the words slowly making their way out of my mouth.

"Impressive."

"And since he is so well-connected to the people who run the Russian government, he's a very valuable asset," I said, deep in thought.

"He has the potential to be one of the most valuable assets in history," Hedaya said.

"But you and the Feds are starting to get worried that Alexi might be playing them, right?"

"Remarkable," Hedaya said. "Are you sure you wouldn't like to join one of the agencies? I could make a few calls."

"No, thanks," I said, shaking my head. "I'd miss the dogs too much. Besides, this stuff is just a hobby."

"Stamp collecting is a hobby," Hedaya said. "This is something else altogether."

"I guess you're right," I said. "So, you'd like me to snoop around while I'm here and poke the bear when I get a chance."

"Yes, but you'll need to remember that it is the Russian bear you'll be poking," he said. "Try not to get too far, oh, what's the expression I'm looking for?"

"Too far over my skis?"

"That's the one."

"Is the list of people who might be somehow involved the same as the people who were at dinner last night?"

"Pretty much," Hedaya said, draining the last of his champagne.

"Natalie?"

"Perhaps," he said with a frown. "But doubtful."

"I should probably try to have a chat with Alexi."

"If you can find him, yes. But I'm afraid he's gone underground after the events of last night," Hedaya said.

"How about the people who were sitting at the other end of the dinner table?"

"Yes. It's possible that one or more of the performers from Kremlin Heights could be involved."

"Including the two bleached-blonde aerialists?" I said.

"Especially those two," he said, nodding. "And don't let their public demeanor fool you."

"Public demeanor?" I said, frowning at him.

"They do everything they can to come across as dumber than a box of rocks," Hedaya said. "And Kosiny is. But Olga is extremely intelligent. They are both very dangerous people."

"Really? From what I saw backstage after the show, the only thing on their mind seemed to be each other."

"They are both active Russian intelligence agents," Hedaya said. "But since they always come across as dumb and horny, no one pays much attention to what they're actually doing here."

"And what exactly are they doing?" I said, confused.

"Trying to do as much damage as they can to the government," Hedaya said.

"Which one?" I said, scowling.

"That remains to be seen," he said, shrugging. "Like the Chinese are fond of saying, may you live in interesting times."

"Yeah, no problem there," I said, nodding. "So, you're not sure who the blondes are working for?"

"Well, I know they're working for the Russians. But the jury is still out whether or not they are also working for us."

"Weird," I said, shaking my head. "How the heck did you get involved in stuff like this, Hedaya?"

"That is a very long story," he said, giving me a coy smile.

"But you can't tell it to me, right?"

"No, unfortunately, that won't be possible."

"But Summerman, Doc, and Merlin know," I said.

"Of course. It wouldn't be possible for them to do their work if they didn't."

"Okay," I said, slapping my thighs and getting to my feet. "Just how much danger am I going to be in?"

"You shouldn't be in any danger, Suzy. As long as you don't-"

"Get too far over my skis?" I said, raising an eyebrow at him.

"I was going to say piss off the wrong people, but you get the point."

Chapter 15

I did my best to ignore the hostile stare Josie was giving me as we took another synchronized step closer to the enormous doorman who was wearing enough cologne to kill both of us. Josie paused when she got a good whiff, bobbed her head a few times, then sneezed loud enough to draw the attention of several people standing in line near the entrance to Club X. Josie couldn't miss the looks of disdain she was receiving then shrugged.

"Sorry," she said, glancing back and forth at the expectant clubgoers; men predominantly clad in black and most of the women wearing skirts shorter than how I wore my towel getting out of the shower. "Cologne Fever. I think it's terminal."

She received sympathetic nods from a few people in line, and one of the women standing nearby placed a hand on her shoulder and raised her voice to be heard above the relentless thump of the techno leaking outside into the hallway.

"I'm so sorry," the woman said, swaying gently back and forth with a glazed look on her face. "I had an auntie who died from that."

"Really?" Josie said, staring at the young woman in disbelief.

"Yeah, I think that was it," she said, deep in thought. "It was just *awful*. How long have you got?"

"What?" Josie said, leaning her head closer to the woman.

"I said, how long have you got?"

114

"Oh. Judging by the look of things, I'll be lucky if I make it through the night," Josie said as she took another look around, cringing at the music. Then she fixed another death stare on me. "What on earth are we doing here?"

"Reconnaissance," I said, unsuccessfully trying to pick up the beat and bop along with the music that had transitioned into a style I believed was called industrial. I wasn't sure what the primary instruments used to play it were, but it sounded like banging metal pipes and blaring car horns were featured. "Relax, it'll be fun."

I glanced over at Millie and Jill who were still basking in the glow of winning again at craps. Given the fact that my mother had helped both of them each win around ten grand, they would have been happy sitting in the parking lot. Chef Claire and Louie were standing behind them and trying to carry on a conversation. Then they finally shrugged at each other and gave up.

When we reached the head of the line, the doorman looked up from the clipboard he was holding and gave us the once-over.

"Can I help you?" the doorman said, lingering on Josie longer than necessary.

"Hi," I said, trying unsuccessfully to shake my shoulders in time to the music. "We're supposed to meet the Russian Heights crew here."

It was the doorman's turn to frown.

"Really?" he said, then broke into a grin as he glanced back and forth at us. "You're hanging out with the aerialists? Sorry, I'm afraid you'll have to do better than that."

115

"What?" I said, staring back at him.

"The excuse you're using to convince me to let you in," he said, tapping his clipboard with his pen. "No offense, but I don't think this is your kind of place. But there's a Neil Diamond tribute band playing in the lounge on the main floor that might be more your style." He grinned at me again. "You ladies can bump and grind as you sweat to the oldies."

"Bump and grind?"

"Yeah, you must remember what it's like to do the old bump and grind," he said, laughing.

"Okay, so that's the way you want to play it, huh?" I said, glancing at Josie. "I don't think I like him very much."

"Well, you always were a great judge of character," Josie said, fixing her glare on the doorman.

"Look, maybe I'll be able to squeeze you in around 1:30. You know, if it's not past your bedtime." He flashed me a crocodile smile I so wanted to knock off his face. Then he spotted the freezer burn poking through my concealer and nodded at it. "What happened to your face?"

"Bar fight," I said. "Now, why don't you take another look at your clipboard and tell us where we can find the folks from Russian Heights?"

"Nah, I'm not going to do that," he said, shaking his head. "Now, if you wouldn't mind taking a step to the side. You're holding up the line."

"Actually, I think you're the one who's holding it up," I said, maintaining solid eye contact.

"Look, lady," he said, getting annoyed. "Are you sure you're in the right place?"

"Great question," Josie said, nodding.

"I think this is the place," I said, forcing a smile at him before glancing over at Josie. "Didn't Hedaya tell us to take the elevator to the 35th floor and then look for the doorman with the cement head?"

"Hey," he said, offended. Then he subconsciously rubbed his bald head. "There's no need to be rude." Then the penny dropped. "Wait a sec. Did you say Hedaya invited you up here?"

I slowly nodded my head as I beamed at him.

"You're friends with Hedaya?"

"We are," I said, nodding. "Actually, I'm doing some work for him at the moment."

"Doing what?"

"I'm conducting an audit on how well his staff treats the customers," I said, leaning close to read his name tag. "Thomas."

I beamed at him and waited for him to fold. Beaten, he pulled the rope back and waved us in.

"They're in the VIP section. Back corner on the right," he said, glancing off into the crowd.

We entered the club, and the music amped up to a decibel level that rivaled a jet engine in full roar. An enormous U-shaped bar ringed the room and a multi-colored light show flashed and flickered as several hundred people bounced up and down on the dance floor as the music transitioned again. This time into a droning pulse propelled by drums and synthesizers that produced a strange cross-sense image: It *sounded* like what having your wisdom teeth pulled *felt* like. We worked out way along the far wall past a section of the bar where bartenders were frantically trying to keep up with the drink orders. I came to a stop in front of a raised section that was cordoned off from the rest of the club. Another man holding a clipboard stared at us as we approached.

"Here we go again," I said, shaking my head.

"What?" Josie yelled.

"Never mind," I said, then beamed at the man who obviously controlled access to the VIP section. "We're with the Russian Heights group."

The man pulled the strand of velvet rope back and gestured us in. We climbed the short set of steps and spotted Wanda sitting in the back with about ten other people. She saw me and waved. The volume of the music faded enough to enable us to speak without damaging our vocal chords. Two staff members arranged some additional chairs around the large round table, and I sat down between the two bleached blonde aerialists. They both looked at me, then remembered my face from dinner the previous evening.

"Olga and Kosiny, right?" I said, glancing back and forth at them.

"That's us," Olga said, extending her hand. "Suzy?"

"Good memory," I said, returning the handshake. "Great show tonight."

"Oh, you were there," she said, apparently pleased to make a new fan. "Yes, it went well." Then she gave Kosiny a quick glare. "Apart from someone forgetting to clip his fingernails."

"Let it go," Kosiny said, then drained the last half of his champagne.

I smiled up at the server who was pouring my champagne, then took a sip and a quick glance around the table before focusing my thoughts on the task at hand.

Showtime.

"It must have been difficult performing tonight," I said. "You know, given what happened to Sergei last night."

Olga and Kosiny glanced at each other as if deciding which one of them would respond. Olga went first.

"It was," she said, staring down at the table. "But what can you do? The show must go on, right?"

"Sure, sure."

"Such a loss," Olga said as her eyes welled with tears.

I had no idea if her tears were genuine or not. But if she could conjure tears up at the drop of a hat, she was very good at it.

"Tragic," Kosiny said, holding out his glass for a refill.

I remembered Wanda's comment about how she and Sergei had once been an item and was curious to see if she'd be willing to share that tidbit with me.

"Did you know him well?" I said, glancing back and forth at them.

"Of course," Olga said. "The Russian community here may be small, but we're a very close-knit group."

"I get that," I said, nodding. "You're all a long way from home."

"Not really," Kosiny said. "I live here."

"She was talking about the Motherland," Olga said, rolling her eyes at him.

"Oh, right," he said, nodding. "Yes, we're a long way from home."

The guy's reputation for being an idiot was apparently spot on. I sat quietly trying to figure out a way to steer the conversation in the direction of how they spent their spare time when they weren't somersaulting through the air or making out backstage.

"How long did it take you to learn all those things you do in the show?" I said, deciding to play it safe until a better question came along.

"Years," Kosiny said, quickly working his way through his fresh glass of champers.

"Did you study in Russia?"

"Yes," he said, nodding without making eye contact.

"We were both at the Moscow School for Performing Arts," Olga said.

"And then you moved here?"

"Eventually," she said, taking a small sip. "The opportunity to work here in the States was too good to pass up."

"Do you often get a chance to get back home?" I said, staying casual.

"Often enough," she said. "Once or twice a year."

"Nice," I said, nodding. I was shooting blanks, so I decided to shift gears. "It was quite a collection at dinner last night."

"What do you mean?" Olga said, suddenly edgy and paying close attention.

"Well, there were so many different people at the table. And all of them doing some very interesting things."

"Interesting?" she said, leaning back in her chair. "How so?"

"It just seemed to be such an interesting collection of people. There were you and the other performers. And you're all amazingly talented."

They both smiled at the compliment and seemed to nod in agreement.

"And Sergei, rest his soul, was fascinating. I mean, who would have ever thought that people would enjoy sitting in a freezer eating caviar and drinking vodka?"

"You have no idea how cold it is inside that place," Olga said, shivering at the memory.

"I could probably ballpark it."

"What?"

"Nothing," I said, then continued. "Sergei must have been an amazing businessman. So smart and creative."

"He was," Kosiny said, nodding in agreement and listening closely to what I was saying.

"And the man sitting across the table from me is obviously very successful as well," I said, tossing my line in the water. "I can't remember his name."

"Alexi," Olga said.

"That's it," I said, nodding. "He's in oil, right?"

"Among other things," Kosiny said, swirling the champagne in his glass and studying the bubbles.

"He's not here tonight?" I said, glancing around the table.

"No, Alexi doesn't like to mingle with our kind," Olga said, laughing.

"I beg your pardon," I said, focusing on her.

"Alexi considers us beneath his station in life," she said. "To him, we're no different than a trained, dancing bear."

"And not nearly as entertaining," Kosiny said, tossing back what was left in his glass.

"Harsh," I said, shaking my head.

"It's not a problem," Kosiny said, glancing around for signs of our server. "Alexi's day is coming."

Olga leaned forward and placed a hand on his, apparently to make him stop talking.

"I'm tired, Kosiny," she said, giving him a look I couldn't miss. "Why don't we head back to your room?"

Kosiny nodded vigorously and immediately got to his feet. Trained dancing bear indeed.

122

"It was nice seeing you again, Suzy," Olga said, beaming at me. "How long will you be in town?"

"Until Sunday."

"Maybe we'll see you again before you go," she said, taking Kosiny by the hand.

"That would be nice," I said with a wave as they headed for the exit.

I continued to watch them until they disappeared from sight and was about to slide into the vacant chair next to Wanda when I realized Kosiny's seat was already occupied.

"Natalie?" I said, frowning. "Where the heck did you come from?"

"A small town outside of Leningrad," she said, grabbing a glass and helping herself to champagne.

"Good to know," I said, confused. "But what I meant was-"

"I know what you meant," she said, taking a sip. "I've been around most of the evening."

"Spying?" I said, going for funny.

"Amateurs spy," she said, taking another sip before setting her glass down. "Professionals study."

"Okay," I said, nodding. "Can I ask you a question?"

"Since when do you feel the need to ask for permission?" she said, giving me an odd look.

"Professional courtesy, I guess," I said, shrugging.

She kept staring at me. I took it as an invitation to proceed.

"I couldn't help but notice that you seem very...severe."

"Severe," she said, giving it some thought. "I suppose that is an accurate description."

"So, what's the deal?"

"Deal?"

"Yeah, why the long face? Most of the time you seem to walk around looking like your dog died."

"Unfortunately, given my job, it's not possible for me to have a dog," she said, shrugging. "I haven't had a dog since I was a young girl."

"That's so sad," I said, unable to grasp the concept of a life without a whole bunch of the four-legged wonders at my feet. "Back when you were a girl in the small town outside of Leningrad?"

"Yes."

"What happened?"

"I began my training and was forced to say goodbye to my dog. His name was Uri."

"You started training to be a spy when you were a young girl?"

"I did," she said, nodding as she drifted away on a memory.

"Can I ask you another question?"

"You certainly are an inquisitive creature, aren't you?"

"Yeah, I really need to start working on that," I said, then continued. "Why are you so upfront with everyone about the fact you're a spy?"

"Everyone around here knows I'm a spy," she said, shrugging. "What's the point of trying to deny it?"

"But doesn't that bother your handlers?" I said.

"My handlers?" she said, letting loose with a sound that approached laughter. "What makes you think I have handlers?"

"I just assumed. Don't all spies have them?"

"I used to have someone who *thought* she handled me," Natalie said. "But as she soon discovered, the reality was quite different."

"Okay," I said, thoroughly confused. "But don't you worry about something happening to you?"

"Like what?" she said, casually taking a sip of champagne.

"I don't know," I said, shrugging. "Like getting shot. Or thrown in front of a bus."

"No, I do not worry about that."

"Because you know where all the bodies are buried, right?" I said, again going for lighthearted because the woman's blasé demeanor was starting to make me nervous.

"A lot of them, yes," she said, glancing around. "But it's a big desert out there. Do you think I can get away with smoking a cigarette in here?"

"You'll get no argument from me."

She lit her cigarette and blew smoke up at the ceiling. Our server spotted the smoke and headed straight for our table. But he stopped when he recognized Natalie and raised his palms and walked away.

125

"Who are you?" I said, unable to take my eyes off her.

"What do you mean?" she said, taking a long drag and exhaling.

"I just can't believe you're so open about what you do," I said. "And as soon as the server saw that it was you who was smoking, he turned tail and scurried off."

"He knows who I work for," she said, taking a sip of champagne.

"And who's that?"

"The same person you're working for," she said, locking eyes with me.

"You work for Hedaya?"

"Yes," she said through a cloud of smoke.

Chapter 16

Josie and I left the club about an hour later trailed by Chef Claire and Louie. Millie and Jill, still on a high from their good fortune at the craps table, stayed behind to dance and burn off some of the adrenaline. I took a final glance back at the dance floor and spotted their heads bouncing up and down in the middle of the throng.

"Nice place," I said to the bald doorman who continued to guard entry to the palace.

"You had a good time?" he said, surprised.

"Most productive," I said as I brushed past him with a finger wave.

"That was brutal," Louie said, trying to unblock his ears.

We headed for the elevators. I pressed the down button and waited patiently for it to arrive.

"That woman gives me the creeps," Josie said. "What were you talking about?"

"I'm really not sure," I said, frowning as I remembered my strange conversation with Natalie. "It was weird. You never give it a second thought when somebody tells you they're a doctor or an accountant, but when someone comes right out and tells you she's a spy, it really catches you off guard."

"Maybe that's why she does it," Josie said, glancing around at the crowd that was holding strong even though it was after two.

127

"Maybe," I said, shrugging. "She says she works for Hedaya. How is that possible?"

"A Russian spy working for a Chinese casino owner?" she said. "I suppose I can make that work."

"It's part of Natalie's schtick," Louie said, stepping back to let people get off the elevator.

"You know her?" I said.

"Sure, everybody knows Natalie," he said. "She's a total burnout. I don't think she's been a spy for at least ten years, but everybody seems to humor her."

"I'm not following," I said, getting on the elevator.

"I think people kind of feel sorry for her," Louie said. "The word on the street is that she washed out several years ago. And now people tolerate her hanging around."

"Or they leave her alone because she has a lot of damaging information people don't want to get out?" I said.

"I suppose that's possible," Louie said, giving it some thought. "But she's pretty harmless. I think Hedaya gives her some projects to work on from time to time just to keep her occupied. Natalie is kind of like a local attraction around the casino. So, he encourages her to make herself known and talk to the guests to add some mystery to the place. It's so Hedaya."

Louie laughed and shook his head.

"I think she's weird," Josie said, scratching the bandage on her arm.

"Don't scratch it. Just leave it alone."

128

"Easy for you to say," she said, going after it like one of our dogs goes after a flea.

"At least it's starting to itch," I said. "That's a good sign."

"So, what's next on your agenda?" Chef Claire said, glancing at her watch.

"I'm thinking about heading back to the suite," Josie said.

"Room service and a movie?" I said.

"Perfect," she said, nodding. "How about you two? You want to join us?"

"Uh, I thought we might…go for a walk," Chef Claire said, blushing.

I glanced at Josie and we exchanged knowing smiles.

"Okay," Josie said, laughing. "You kids have fun on your *walk*."

"Don't start," Chef Claire said, doing her best to keep a straight face.

"Too late," Josie said.

The elevator came to a stop, and we exited and waved to them, grinning the entire time. We headed down the hall, and I inserted the keycard in the slot and opened the door. My mother was stretched out on one of the couches eating popcorn and watching a movie.

"Don't you ever sleep?" I said, digging into the bowl of popcorn.

"I'm too keyed up," she said, pausing the movie.

"Yeah, Millie and Jill are the same," I said. "How much did you end up winning?"

"A lot," she said with a big grin.

"Good for you, Mom," I said, giving her a quick hug before reaching for another handful. "What are you watching?"

"*The Usual Suspects*," she said, making room on the couch for us. "Have a seat. It just started."

"Great," Josie said, plopping down on the couch and tucking her legs underneath her. She helped herself to the bowl of popcorn my mother was holding out. "One of my favorites. I never saw the hook at the end coming the first time I watched it."

"Me either," my mother said, then caught the look on my face.

"What is it, darling?"

"I'm just wondering what sort of hook is behind all this," I said, grabbing a bottle of water and chugging.

"Why don't you just relax and enjoy the weekend?" my mother said, briefly taking her eyes off the screen.

"Sure, sure," I said, staring out at the night sky.

"Forget I said anything," she said, then went back to the movie.

"What's that, Mom?"

Chapter 17

Friday

At ten the next morning, after an hour in the sun interspersed with quick dips in the pool, I left the spaniels with Josie and Jill under a cabana and headed for Hedaya's office. After my conversation last night with the aerialists, Olga and Kosiny, followed by my chat with Natalie, my Snoopmeter had redlined and stayed that way the rest of the night. And by the time we had finished watching the movie, a classic about misdirection and alternate realities, I began to wonder if the casino owner was being straight with me. So, on four hours of sleep and after half a lap in the pool, I headed inside to have a conversation with the old man and get a few questions answered.

As I walked down a long hallway that eventually led to the registration area, I replayed what I knew in my head. Sergei, the owner of the infamous vodka bar, was dead. I made a mental note to ask Hedaya if the official cause of death had been confirmed. The fact that the dead Russian had been found inside Bugsy's enclosure continued to nag at me. Since the glass wall separating the lizard from the rest of us was about ten feet high, I wondered if two people had been required to lift him over the wall. Unless Sergei had somehow gained access to the lizard's home using one of the two access cards Hedaya had mentioned. I made another mental note to figure out a way to have a chat with the keeper of

131

the second access card, the person responsible for the care and feeding of Bugsy.

I walked past a frazzled couple arguing about whether to have breakfast or an early lunch. I doubted if food was at the core of their argument. More likely was the possibility that they'd had a run of bad luck at the tables and were more comfortable fighting about omelets versus prime rib than how they were going to replenish junior's college fund or make next month's mortgage. And since their conversation was obviously getting heated, in the interest of promoting marital accord, I casually tossed out a suggestion as I passed them.

"Have the buffet," I said without slowing down.

I frowned at my ongoing ease at interjecting myself into things that were absolutely no business of mine and wondered again if that was why Hedaya had wanted me involved. I was basically a stranger to him. And despite the fact that my mother had spoken with pride about my snooping abilities, something she never did in my presence, and that those abilities had been confirmed by other people Hedaya knew and trusted, it still seemed odd that a man with his resources and contacts would want someone like me poking the bear.

The Russians I'd met so far were definitely an odd bunch. The bleached blonde aerialists came across as ego-driven performers who were obviously enjoying their local standing as fringe celebrities. But Olga and Kosiny had an edge lurking just below the surface that was off-putting, to say the least. And

Natalie, the dour ex-spy, was in a class all by herself as, what Josie was calling, the founder and sole member of Club Weird. A former spy who might still be an active agent, an acerbic woman who openly talked about her profession, and, if Louie could be believed, was basically the casino's mascot.

I had no idea if any of them had been responsible for Sergei's death, but I was quite sure both aerialists had the physical strength to lift the dead Russian over the glass wall. And Natalie's personality might have been enough to cause Sergei to climb the wall just to get away from her.

I continued down the hallway and chastised myself for taking such a cheap shot at the woman. I barely knew her, and she'd been nice enough to me both times I'd interacted with her. But Josie was right. Natalie was definitely an odd duck. And like a duck, I was sure, despite the cool demeanor she put on display, beneath the surface she was paddling like crazy.

I then focused on what I needed to do today before four o'clock when we had tickets for a matinee performance featuring one of my mother's all-time favorite singers. Tommy Mandolin was someone I had grown up listening to around the house. Actually, listening to is a bit of a stretch since every time my mother put one of his CDs on, I invariably headed upstairs to my room and blasted Zeppelin through my headphones to drown out the droning crooner. But my mother continued to be a fan even though his days of touring the country were long over. Several years ago, he had taken up residence in Vegas and now spent his time regaling tourists with his catalog of hits six nights a week with matinee performances on Friday and Saturday.

I checked my watch and determined I had less than six hours before I needed to be in my seat at the show. Before then I needed to talk to Hedaya, then do some looking around to see if I might be able to locate Alexi, the oil thief, who continued to be AWOL since the dinner party. I also wanted to speak with the person responsible for making sure Bugsy led a long, healthy life. And then I remembered another name I'd heard while freezing my butt off in the tasting room. Natalie had mentioned a woman by the name of Maria when she'd been talking to the head of the construction crew. And since she had referenced her name while talking about Sergei, I assumed Maria might have been the dead Russian's current girlfriend.

It was a lot to do in a short period of time, and I doubted if I would be able to get it all done today. I ignored the rumble in my stomach when I stopped in front of the registration desk and informed the clerk that I wanted to speak with Hedaya. She made a call and I was soon escorted to his office. I knocked softly on the door and heard Hedaya invite me in. I stepped inside the office and stared at the two detectives who were sitting across the desk from the obviously distressed casino owner.

"Good morning, Suzy," Hedaya said, getting to his feet and motioning for us to join him in the sitting area.

"Hi, Hedaya," I said, glancing back and forth at Detective Williams and Detective Swan. "I can come back later."

134

"No, please stay," he said, sitting down. "You need to hear this."

"Okay," I said, frowning as I sat down on a couch. "Hello, Detectives. How are you guys doing?"

"We've had better mornings," Detective Williams said, jotting down a note.

"What's going on?" I said to Hedaya.

"I'm afraid there's been another...incident," the old man said, running a hand through his hair.

"Who's dead?"

"What makes you think someone's dead?" Detective Williams said, cocking his head at me.

I ignored the suspicious look he was giving me.

"Let's call it a hunch," I said.

Detective Swan stifled a laugh that drew a stern look of rebuke from her partner.

"It's Kosiny," Hedaya said, obviously still stunned by the news.

"Kosiny is dead?" I said. "I just saw him at Club X last night."

"Interesting," Detective Williams said.

"Not really," I said with a shrug. "He's not much of a conversationalist. Or I guess I should say, he wasn't."

"What time did you last see him?" Detective Swan said, her pen poised.

"It must have been around one," I said, then nodded in confirmation. "Yeah, it was just after one. He and Olga said they were going to bed."

"He was with Olga?" Detective Williams said.

"Nothing gets past you, Detective."

"Play nice," Detective Swan said, her voice rising a notch.

"Sorry," I said. "Yes, we were sitting with them and some of the other performers from their show in the VIP section. Then they left." I looked around at all three of them. "What happened to him?"

"He did a header off his balcony," Detective Williams said.

"What?" I said with a deep frown then forced myself to ask the question. "What floor was he on?"

"Twenty-two," Hedaya whispered.

"Geez," I grunted. "Did he land in front of the casino?"

"No, his room faced one of the parking lots in the rear," Hedaya said. "He landed on a Toyota."

"It made a mess of the car," Detective Williams said.

"I can't imagine it did much for Kosiny either," I said. Then I noticed the looks I was receiving from the cops. "Sorry. Just sayin'."

"Did Kosiny seem distressed last night?" Detective Swan said.

"No."

"Angry?"

"Nope."

"Afraid?"

"Not that I noticed," I said, shaking my head.

"Then how did he seem?" Detective Williams said, leaning forward.

I sat quietly with a frown on my face.

"You're holding something back," Detective Williams said.

"No, that's not it," I said, shaking my head. "I'm just trying to remember if there's a technical term for it."

"Don't worry about that," Detective Swan said, her pen again poised. "Just put it in your own words."

"Okay. Actually, Kosiny seemed…horny," I said with a shrug. "Like he was anxious to get out of there so he and Olga could…"

"Got it," Detective Swan said.

"What does Olga have to say about what happened?" I said.

"We don't know," Detective Williams said. "Olga is missing."

"She's gone?" I said, raising an eyebrow.

"Nothing gets past you."

"Funny. Well played, Detective."

Detective Williams grinned at me then turned his attention to Hedaya.

"You don't know where she might have gone?"

"No, I'm afraid I don't," the old man said. "They both have rooms in the hotel, but my understanding is that they've been

137

inseparable since they started dating. And if Olga isn't in her room, I wouldn't have a clue where she might be."

"She's not there," Detective Swan said. "But I'm sure she'll turn up. Unless she was somehow involved in the murder."

"Assuming he was murdered," Detective Williams said.

"I doubt very much if he jumped," Detective Swan said, turning to her partner.

"It does seem odd," he said. "Unless it was an accident and he fell."

"A world-class aerialist falling off a balcony?" I said to myself more than anyone else.

"Maybe he was showing off for his girlfriend," Detective Williams said.

"Something like, *Hey, Honey, watch me do a handstand on this railing?*" I said, staring at him.

"It's possible," he said, then frowned. "But not very likely."

"Is there anything else at the moment?" Hedaya said, glancing back and forth at the two cops.

"No, I think that's it for now, Hedaya," Detective Williams said, getting to his feet. "But we may have some additional questions later on."

"Of course," Hedaya said, extending his hand. "Just let me know."

The detectives shook hands with him and gave me a wave on their way out the door. Hedaya sat back down and rubbed his forehead.

138

"Most perplexing," he said, draping a leg over his knee.

"Did you tell them about the key?"

"I did not," he said, jiggling his foot. "This certainly adds another layer to the mystery."

"What mystery is that?"

"The mystery of what the hell is going on around here," he said, staring off at the wall. Then he shook his head as if to clear it and focused on me. "What did you need to see me about?"

"I need some questions answered," I said, leaning back on the couch.

"Don't we all?" he said, then stared at me. "What do you need to know?"

"Well, for starters, how about you come clean with me?"

He stared at me for several moments, then nodded.

"Okay. Let's chat."

Chapter 18

Hedaya poured coffee for both of us then sat back and sipped in silence. Eventually, he made eye contact and shrugged.

"Should I just start talking or would you like to ask questions?"

"Maybe I should go first," I said. Then he nodded and gestured for me to get the ball rolling. "Okay, let's start with a big one. Why on earth did you ask me to get involved with this situation? Whatever the heck it is."

"Fair enough," he said, nodding. "Because I need some information. And I've learned over the years is that it's often easier to get information when people have their guard down. And since you're an outsider, no one would expect you to be involved."

"Natalie knows."

"Only because I told her," Hedaya said, glancing at me over the top of his coffee cup.

"So, she does work for you?"

"She does," he said, nodding.

"I'm confused, Hedaya," I said, leaning forward. "Why does she make it a point to tell everyone what she does? Or used to do? Or maybe even wished she did? I'm at a loss to explain her behavior."

"And that's just the way we like it," he said with a grin.

I stared at him and waited for more.

140

"Everyone who knows Natalie is convinced that she is a total burnout who possibly used to be a spy and is merely regaling visitors with her stories and trying to relive the glory days. You've probably already heard people talk about how she is a hanger-on. Someone I tolerate having around because she adds a bit of mystery and some color to the place."

"Mascot was the term I heard," I said, sipping my coffee.

"That works," Hedaya said. "But I can assure you that Natalie is far from burned out. In fact, she is one of the sharpest people I've ever met."

"So, she still is an active agent," I said.

"Very much so."

"Working for the Russians?"

"No, absolutely not," he said, shaking his head. "As far as the Russians are concerned, Natalie is very much retired and a tragic case of what can happen to someone who chooses that profession. A cautionary tale, if you will."

"Okay," I said, nodding. "So, she's working for us. I mean, the Americans."

"No," he said, again shaking his head. "As far as the Americans are concerned, Natalie is completely off their radar. While they don't share the pity her associates have for her, they, too, believe that she is simply an old intelligence officer who's been put out to pasture. And since she never gets entangled in any U.S. versus Russia situations, they rarely pay any attention to her."

"I gotta tell you, Hedaya. That sounds a bit hard to believe."

"Not really," he said. "It's like an old friend told me one time about his days as a reluctant member of the Army Reserves. He said the key to making his time in the service as easy as possible was to never volunteer and when asked if he knew how to do something to always say no. Over time, whenever his sergeant was looking for people to assign a task to, he would call everyone together and walk down the line of troops. Every time he spotted Jeff, he would say out loud, 'Nope, you don't know how to do it.' Then he would move on down the line."

"I used a similar strategy in gym class," I said with a shrug.

"Good for you," Hedaya said, laughing. "Natalie uses the same approach. Over time, people have just gotten used to ignoring her. It's like she's part of the furniture."

"Got it," I said, nodding at what seemed to make some sense. "But if she's not working for us or the Russians, who the heck is she working for?"

"She works for me," he said, setting his empty coffee cup down.

"Yes, I know that, Hedaya. But to what end? There must be a bigger play going on around here."

Hedaya stared at me for a long time. Then he checked to make sure his office door was closed before focusing on me.

"Okay, I guess you need to know. I'm about to tell you something that you can't repeat to *anyone*, *ever*," he said without emotion. "Unless you decide right now that you don't want to hear it. If you don't, that's fine. You can head back out to the pool and

142

enjoy the rest of your time here hanging out with your mother and friends."

He gave me a dead-eyed look that made the hairs on the back of my neck tingle.

"I can't tell anybody?"

"No. And that is *not* negotiable."

"This oughta be good," I said, leaning forward in my chair. "Do Summerman and Doc and Merlin know what you're talking about?"

"They do. And they are all heavily involved in it," he said.

"And the reason you asked for my help is because they're busy doing other things at the moment?" I said, treading carefully.

"Partially, yes," Hedaya said. "But I am always on the lookout for additional *participants,* and you come highly recommended."

"By whom?"

"All three of them. But primarily, Doc. I value his opinion almost as much as I do my own."

"Okay," I said, then forced myself to ask the question when a thought surfaced. "Does my mother know about this?"

"No, of course not," he said. "But I'm sure she would be more than supportive of our cause if she was in the loop."

"Your cause? You're starting to freak me out a bit here, Hedaya."

"That wasn't my intent," he said, laughing

"So, back to my earlier question," I said, staring hard at him. "Who does Natalie work for? Apart from you, that is?"

"Is that your way of saying you'd like to know more?" he said, raising an eyebrow at me.

"What can I say? You've piqued my interest."

"Okay. But I must remind you that you can never breathe a word of this to anyone."

"Hey, I once had Billy Johnson in my room all weekend during my senior year, and my mother still doesn't know to this day."

"I'm afraid this is a bit more dangerous than keeping a secret from your mother about what you were doing with an old boyfriend," he said.

"Have you met my mother?" I said, laughing. "C'mon Hedaya. Natalie. Who's she working for?"

"For the Chinese Democratic Front," he whispered.

I sat back and stared at him as I tried to process that little nugget.

"Man, I wouldn't have gotten that with a million guesses."

I remained baffled and waited for him to continue.

"I assume you've heard my personal story," he said.

"Bits and pieces of it. My mother mentioned that you were orphaned at a young age, then somehow managed to get out of China and make your way to the States. You started with nothing, and over the years, you became a billionaire."

"Yes," he said with a small smile as the memories washed over him.

"A classic rags to riches story."

"An *American* story," he said, sounding like he was almost correcting me.

"Fair enough," I said, deep in thought. "So, this Chinese Democratic Front is some sort of organization working to overthrow the Communists in the hope of turning China democratic?"

"Overthrow is such a strong word," he said, refilling our coffee cups. "But you get the general idea."

"How the heck are you going to do that?" I said.

"That is one area we won't be discussing," he said, waving it off. "It would simply be too dangerous for you."

"More dangerous than snooping around a bunch of Russians?"

"Much more dangerous," Hedaya said, then noticed the deep frown on my face. "What's the matter?"

"I'm just thinking," I said. "You must have been working with this organization for a long time, right?"

"I have," he said, nodding. "In fact, I founded it. Almost thirty years ago."

"Are you CIA, Hedaya?"

"Oh, my, no," he said, laughing. "But our paths do intersect at times."

"Doc and Merlin, right?"

145

"It wouldn't be fair to them to say. So, I'll neither confirm nor deny."

"Okay," I said, continuing to wait for my neurons to coalesce. "Thirty years is a long time."

"Not really," Hedaya said. "Change of that magnitude requires a long time to take root."

"And a lot of money," I said, glancing at him.

"Indeed."

Then a lightbulb popped.

"You're using the casino to launder money, aren't you?"

"Now you sound like the FBI," he said, laughing as he walked to his desk. He made a quick phone call and then sat back down.

"You've got a network of people working in China, and you and some of your friends are funding it by using the casino to move the money," I said, nodding. "I'm right, aren't I?"

"I'm impressed."

"Lucky guess," I said, shrugging it off. "And the U.S. intelligence agencies know what you're doing?"

"Let's say there are a handful of the right people who know," he said. "They're in full agreement with what we're trying to do, but for *political* reasons, it's best that our operation stays way below the radar."

"A democratic China?" I said, shaking my head. "I'm certainly no expert when it comes to global politics, but that sounds like a long shot, Hedaya."

"So was the fall of the Soviet Union," he said softly.

"The Russians," I said, perking up. "You need to know if the Russians have figured out what you're doing in China."

"You are good."

"Thanks," I said, waving it off as I concentrated. "You're worried that, given the recent Russian reemergence as a global power, they're looking for ways to ingratiate themselves with the Chinese government."

"Remarkable," Hedaya whispered.

"And if the Russians could uncover a plot designed to delegitimize the Chinese government that has, at a minimum, the tacit approval of the U.S. government, the people who run China would be extremely grateful."

"Yes," he said, nodding. "And then they would kill thousands of people who support our democratic objectives."

"Not to mention the fact that you'd potentially have the two biggest autocratic governments on the planet working together," I said, then glanced at him for confirmation. "That's one of the biggest concerns our government has, right?"

"It's certainly high on the list," he said. "Russia and China working in tandem to install even more autocratic puppets in various places around the world is something that must be avoided at all costs."

"Does the CIA know what the Russians might be doing here?"

"If they do, they haven't shared it with me. But I doubt it," he said, shaking his head. "At the moment, I'm not even sure I know what they're doing."

"The key," I said, sitting up straight on the couch. "The key is the key, right?"

"How do you say it?" Hedaya said with a grin.

"What?"

"That saying I've heard you use," he said, laughing. "Nothing gets past you?"

"That's the one," I said, grinning back at him. "You need to find out what that key opens and figure out if the Russians have discovered information about your underground organization."

"Yes, I do."

"And if the Russians have somehow hacked into your records, they're only one step away from sharing it with the Chinese, and it would be goodbye Chinese Democratic Front."

"And also, goodbye Hedaya," he said, cocking his head at me.

I leaned back into the couch and put my feet up on the coffee table.

"This is an awful lot to process."

"You asked," he said with a shrug.

"Geez, Hedaya," I said, wiggling my toes. "How the heck did you get yourself into this mess?"

"It's merely one of the occasional bumps in the road our organization has to deal with."

"No, I meant you," I said, glancing over at him. "I would have expected you to be kicking back by now and enjoying the life you've built."

"Don't worry," he said, smiling. "I certainly enjoy myself. But it's important work. What else should I be doing?"

"I don't know," I said. "At your age, I suppose eating soup and yelling at people to get off the lawn."

Hedaya laughed long and hard then we both glanced at the door when we heard the knock.

"Come in," Hedaya called out.

Natalie entered the office and closed the door behind her.

"You wanted to see me?" she said, nodding hello to me.

"I did," he said, still chuckling. "Please, have a seat."

She did and focused her attention on the old man.

"I wanted to let you know that I decided to ask Suzy for some additional help with our current situation," he said.

"Why did you do that?" Natalie said, scowling.

"Because we need to have some conversations with our *friends*, and I can't think of any other way to do it."

"Torture is always a good option," Natalie said without emotion.

"Perhaps another time," he said, raising an eyebrow at her. "But I think we should start by talking."

"I haven't been able to get a word out of them," she said.

"Neither have I," Hedaya said. "That's why I thought Suzy might be able to help us out."

"Why would they open up to a complete stranger?" Natalie said, then glanced at me. "No offense."

"None taken," I said, stifling a yawn.

"We were just about to get to that," Hedaya said, then remembered something. "Oh, did you hear about Kosiny?"

"Yes, I'm aware of the situation," she said with a small smile. "Tragic."

"Not really," Hedaya said, shrugging it off. "I never liked Kosiny."

"Nobody did," Natalie said.

"Not even Olga?" I said, glancing over at her.

"Not even Olga," she said, staring back.

"That's odd," I said. "You know, since they were…"

"Just part of the job," Natalie said, then stared at the wall. "Not a part of the job I've ever enjoyed."

"Yeah, I get that," I said.

"So, Suzy," Hedaya said. "Let me put you on the spot. Do you have any ideas about how we might start collecting some information? I know you only have a few more days here and time is not on our side. If you could at least give us something to work with until some other people can get back to Vegas, I would truly appreciate it."

"I do have an idea," I said, nodding.

"Really?" he said, surprised. "Do tell."

"I thought I'd start with Maria," I said, then glanced back and forth at them to gauge their reaction.

"Maria," Hedaya said, nodding. "That's an interesting choice."

"How do you know about, Maria?" Natalie said, giving me the death stare.

"You mentioned her name," I said, deciding there was no reason to lie to her.

"I did?" she said, frowning.

"Yes, you were talking with Mika. I believe he's the head of the construction crew doing the renovation at Moscow Nights."

"But we were the only ones in the bar," she said, glaring at me. "How on earth did you hear that?"

"I was stuck in the tasting room," I said, shrugging. "And then Mika shut the door and I got locked in."

"Of course," Hedaya said, doing his best not to laugh. "Your adventure in the tasting room."

"Yeah, that's the one," I said, frowning as I gently scratched the freezer burn on the side of my face.

"I should have checked," Natalie said. "But who would be dumb enough to go inside a freezer without backup?"

"I was just exploring," I said. "Backup?"

"You know what I mean," she said, waving it off.

"Maria was Sergei's girlfriend?" I said.

Hedaya and Natalie looked at each other and shrugged in unison.

"She was his latest conquest," Natalie said. "And still a bit of a mystery woman to us."

151

"Then she sounds like someone I should definitely talk to," I said.

"I doubt if she'll have much to say," Natalie said.

"Maybe not," I said. "But I'm sure I'll be able to get something out of her."

"How are you going to do that?" Hedaya said, leaning forward in his chair.

"The dogs."

Chapter 19

I checked in with the gang who were still lounging around the pool, except for my mother who was back at the craps table and apparently determined to bring down Hedaya's financial empire armed with only a pair of dice and a tight-lipped grin. I explained where I was going as I played with the dogs who were stretched out on a double-wide lounger inside the cabana, directly underneath the misting system.

"Tough life you guys lead," I said, scratching both spaniels' ears. "Okay, I'm out of here. I'll be back in time for the matinee."

"Are you sure you don't want company?" Josie said.

"No, I got it," I said. "I'm just going to see if this woman Maria might be interested in taking the dogs."

"Okay," Josie said, lowering her sunglasses to study the look on my face. "Don't do anything crazy."

"Like lose track of time and miss Tommy Mandolin?" I said, laughing as I waved over my shoulder and headed for the main entrance where a town car, courtesy of Hedaya, was waiting for me.

I gave the driver the address then stretched out in the back seat and began formulating a series of questions. I occasionally glanced out the window and noticed we were heading into an upscale neighborhood. I sat up and leaned forward to speak to the driver.

153

"This is a nice area," I said. "Who lives around here?"

"Rich people," he said without taking his eyes off the road.

"Sure, sure."

Deciding that the guy wasn't in a chatty mood, I sat back and enjoyed the rest of the ride. Ten minutes later, he turned into a long driveway and came to a stop outside a gate. He pressed the intercom and moments later I heard a woman's voice.

"Yes? How can I help you?"

"There's someone here who wants to speak with..." he turned around and waited.

"Maria," I said.

"She wants to talk to Maria," the driver said to the intercom.

"I'm Maria," she said, sounding tentative. "Who wants to speak with me?"

"Suzy Chandler," I chirped from the backseat.

"Her name is Suzy Chandler," the driver said.

"I'm sorry, but I don't know a Suzy Chandler," she said. "And I'm quite busy at the moment."

"Hang on," I said, placing a hand on the driver's shoulder. "Tell her it's about Moose and Squirrel."

The driver looked over his shoulder at me with a frown, then shrugged and spoke to the intercom again.

"She wants to talk about a moose and a squirrel," he said, doing his best not to laugh.

"Not a moose and a squirrel," I said. "Moose and Squirrel."

"Sorry," he said, frowning again at me through the rearview mirror. "She wants to talk to you about a couple of guys named Moose and Squirrel."

"Close enough," I whispered, shaking my head.

"Oh, of course," the woman said. "Well, okay. Come on up to the house."

The gate slowly opened and I soon found myself standing in a circular driveway. The house was magnificent, and I spent a few moments admiring the front lawn and gardens I was sure required daily maintenance and a whole lot of water.

"Do you mind waiting?" I said to the driver who was also taking a good look around the property.

"Hey, Hedaya's wish is my command," he said, climbing back into the airconditioned car.

I climbed the short set of steps and pressed the doorbell. Moments later, a barefoot woman wearing shorts and a tee shirt opened the door and stared at me.

"Suzy, right?" she said, giving me an odd look as she peered out the half-opened door.

"Yes, Suzy Chandler," I said, producing my best smile. "You're Maria?"

"I am," she said, still not quite ready to open the door. "How can I help you?"

"Would it be okay to come inside?" I said, already feeling the sweat beading up on my brow. "I think my shoes are melting."

"Oh, of course. I'm so sorry. Come in."

155

I stepped into the massive foyer and glanced around. Italian tile and a ton of ornate furniture that looked really uncomfortable dominated. She led me into what I assumed was the living room and gestured for me to sit down. I did, and she sat down across from me with an expectant look on her face.

"First of all, let me say how sorry I am about Sergei," I said.

"Thank you," she said, not even close to tears. "Did you know him well?"

"No, I only met him once," I said. "Actually, I sat next to him at dinner the night he...died."

I almost said the night he got killed but stopped myself. Then I shrugged when she continued to stare at me.

"He seemed like a good guy."

"He was," she said without emotion. "You said you wanted to talk about the dogs."

"Yes," I said, nodding. "I have them."

"What are you doing with Moose and Squirrel?"

"Good question," I said, then launched into a brief overview about what I did for a living and how we came to be the spaniels' temporary guardian. When I finished, she nodded but continued to sit quietly waiting for me to continue. "So, I thought the right thing to do was to check around to see if there was someone local they should go to."

"I certainly hope you don't expect me to take them," she said, blurting it out. Then her face reddened and she forced a smile. "I mean, I don't think this would be a good place for them."

156

"Yeah, two acres with a pool and an air-conditioned mansion," I said, beginning to dislike her. "What dog would want that?"

"Excuse me?" she said, brushing her hair back from her face.

"Nothing. I take it you're not a dog lover," I said, going for casual.

"Actually, no," she said. "Especially those two."

"What's wrong with them?"

"It's not that there is anything wrong with them," she said, treading carefully. "It's just that they're so...goofy."

"Goofy?" I said, surprised.

"Yes. They're always bouncing around and chasing balls. Craving attention. Drooling. You know, goofy."

"They sound happy to me," I said, shrugging.

"That's what Sergei used to say," she said. "And I hated it when he was working, and I was left alone to keep an eye on them. He was always nagging me about feeding them, making sure they had water, letting them out, letting them in. It never stopped." She sighed heavily. "And don't even get me started on the dog hair."

"The life of a dog owner," I said, nodding.

"Indeed," she said, sitting back in her chair. "I'm afraid it won't be possible for me to take the dogs."

"Geez, there's a surprise," I whispered.

"What?"

"Nothing," I said, shaking my head. "Can you think of anyone else who might want to take them?"

157

She seemed to give my question some serious thought before responding.

"Actually, no," she said. "What do you think is going to happen to them?"

"I imagine they'll live a long and happy life," I said, grinning at her.

"Where?"

"With me," I said.

"I thought you said you already have a lot of dogs."

"We do. But there's always room for more."

"How many do you have?" she said, leaning forward.

"Around seventy at the moment."

"That's a lot of dogs," she said, scowling.

"Yeah, you'd think that," I said, nodding. "But not really."

"Then I guess it's settled," she said. "You can have Moose and Squirrel."

"Perfect," I said, glancing around. "This is a beautiful home. Are you going to be staying here now that Sergei is gone?"

"I'm not sure," she said. "That's going to depend on...some decisions that need to be made in the near future."

"Sure, I get that. With the funeral arrangements, I imagine you have bigger things to deal with at the moment. How long had you and Sergei been living together?"

"Oh, let's see," she said, staring off for a moment. "It was only a few months." Then she stared hard at me to reinforce her next comment. "But we'd gotten very close."

158

"I see," I said. "So, you two started dating right after his relationship with Olga ended?"

She flinched like I'd hit her with a baseball bat.

"Olga?" she whispered.

"Yeah, the tall, bleached blonde aerialist with about two percent body fat."

"I know who she is," Maria said, glaring at me. "But how do you know Olga?"

"Oh, I just met her the other day. We had drinks together at Club X last night."

"I see," she said, suddenly edgy. "I haven't seen her in a while. What did she have to say for herself?"

"Not a lot," I said. "She seemed more focused on getting Kosiny back to their room."

"Okay," she whispered, obviously waiting to see where I was headed.

"I was looking for her this morning," I said.

"You were?"

"Yeah, I wanted to see if there was anything I could do for her. I was worried about how she was holding up after Kosiny's accident."

"What accident?" she said, raising an eyebrow.

"Oh, you haven't heard," I said. "It's terrible." I shook my head and stared down at the tiled floor.

"What happened to Kosiny?"

"He fell off the balcony outside his room."

"He fell from the twenty-second floor?" she said, stunned.

Obviously, this was news to her. What was interesting to me was that she knew what floor his room had been on.

"Yeah, it's tragic," I said. "Apparently, he landed on a Toyota."

For the first time, she showed emotion and her eyes welled with tears.

"How did it happen?"

"Nobody seems to know," I said. "Yet."

I let my comment hang in the air then the silence was broken by noises coming from down the hall. Maria jerked her head in the direction of the sound, seemed to panic briefly, then calmed down and forced a smile at me.

"The housekeeper," she said, lying through her teeth. "She always makes such a racket."

"She does a great job," I said, glancing around the room again. "This place is immaculate."

"If you'll excuse me, I have some…funeral arrangements to take care of," she said, getting to her feet.

"Of course," I said, also standing. "I've taken up enough of your time. Are you sure you're okay with me taking the dogs?"

"Actually, you'll be doing me a favor," she said, glancing down the hall before refocusing on me.

"That's great," I said, rocking back and forth on my heels. "There's just one more thing I'll need."

"What's that?" she said, definitely anxious for me to hit the road.

"I'll just need both dogs' paperwork. You know, ownership, any lineage papers, vaccination records, that sort of thing."

"Certainly," she said. "I believe Sergei kept those in his office. Hang on, I'll be right back."

She quickly headed down the hall and opened a door and disappeared. I tiptoed my way along the tile and came to a stop outside the door. I leaned in and pressed my ear against it. Unless she had two Russian housekeepers, I knew she'd been lying about the noises we'd heard a few minutes earlier.

"She's here about the dogs," Maria whispered.

"Well, get rid of her," a man said. The voice sounded familiar and I eventually put a name to it.

Alexi, the oil thief.

Interesting, I said to myself.

"Why didn't you tell me about Kosiny?" Maria said.

"Tell you what?" a woman whispered back.

Olga.

Also interesting.

"Tell me he was dead," Maria said.

"What?"

"According to the Dog Whisperer, he fell off his balcony," Maria said.

Dog Whisperer?

161

Normally, I'd take that as a compliment, but I don't think that was how she intended it.

"Don't try to tell me you didn't know," Maria said.

"I didn't know," Olga said. "When I left him last night, he was definitely worn out, but he certainly wasn't dead."

"Did you know?" Maria said, apparently shifting her attention to Alexi.

"No," he said. "Are you sure you didn't do it?"

"I think I would know if I threw that idiot off his balcony," Olga snapped.

"Then who the hell did?" Alexi said.

"My guess it was that creature Natalie," Maria said. "She never liked Kosiny."

"She doesn't like anybody," Alexi said. "What on earth are you looking for?"

"The dogs' papers," Maria said as she rummaged through various drawers. "She's not going to leave until she gets them. Where the heck did he keep them?"

"Maybe they're sitting inside whatever that key opens," Olga said.

"Don't even joke about that," Alexi said.

"Here they are," Maria said.

I was just about to do my best lumber back down the hall when I heard Alexi again.

"Olga," he said. "You need to get back to the casino and see what you can find out."

162

"What are you going to do?" she said.

"Uh, Maria and I need to talk about a few things," Alexi said. "Like the possible location of the key."

"Yeah, right," Olga said, laughing.

"Shhh," Maria said.

"Okay, you two have a nice chat," Olga said. "Go get rid of the dog lady so I can get out of here."

I took my cue and did my best lumber back down the hall. When Maria returned holding a thick folder, I was standing in front of the fireplace admiring a painting hanging above the mantel.

"Sorry about that," she said, handing me the folder. "It took me a while to find them."

"Thanks so much," I said. "Is your housekeeper all right?"

"What?" she said, giving me a wide-eyed stare.

"I couldn't help but hear you talking. It sounded like she might be upset."

"Oh, that," she said, her eyes darting back and forth. "I was just telling her about what happened to Kosiny?"

"So, she knew him?"

"Uh, yes, she did. Kosiny would stop by from time to time," Maria said, exhaling loudly. "Now, if you'll excuse me, I should probably have another talk with her to make sure she's okay."

"Of course," I said. "I hope your *talk* helps ease the tension."

"What? Oh, right. Thanks," she said, gesturing toward the front door. "And thanks again for stopping by. I'm sure Moose and Squirrel will be in good hands."

"As will you, right?" I said, not waiting for a response. I gave her an over-the-shoulder finger wave as I headed out to the car.

I climbed into the back seat and glanced at the house. Maria was standing in the doorway with a strange look on her face. Then she closed the door and disappeared from sight.

"Are you ready to go?" my driver said through the rearview mirror.

"I am," I said, grinning.

"Did you get what you came for?"

"I did. And possibly a whole lot more."

Chapter 20

After I got back to the casino, I went looking for Hedaya, and my fruitless search eventually ended on the rooftop. He was nowhere to be found, but I did manage to locate the man responsible for the care and feeding of Bugsy. He was inside the glass enclosure and sitting on a rock tossing chunks of meat that the giant lizard, doing his best dog impression, was snatching out of the air. When he spotted me standing on the other side of the glass, he set the bowl of meat on the ground. He watched Bugsy start working his way through it then stepped outside the enclosure to greet me. He wiped his hands on a towel then we shook hands.

"You're Suzy, right?" he said, giving me a quick once-over. "Hedaya said you'd probably be stopping by. I'm Mercury."

"It's nice to meet you," I said, glancing at the lizard who continued to make short work of his dinner. "How's he doing?"

"He's great," Mercury said, giving the lizard an affectionate look. "And I'd really like to meet your friend and thank her for saving his life."

"She'd like that," I said. "Can I ask you a couple of questions?"

"Sure," he said, sitting down on a large rock and folding his arms across his chest.

"You and Hedaya are the only ones with access cards to the enclosure, right?"

165

"Yes. Hedaya wants to control access as much as he can. Just to protect Bugsy."

"And keep him from eating the tourists," I said, grinning at him.

"That is something we choose not to think about," he said, grinning back.

"And that door is the only way in?"

"It is. At least, officially," he said.

"I'm not following," I said, frowning.

"There are some rocks on the other side of the enclosure," he said, pointing off into the distance. "And it's possible to climb them and get hold of a nearby tree branch. From there, if you're pretty fit, you can scale the glass wall and then jump down."

"I see," I said, giving it some thought. "Has anybody ever tried to do it before?"

"A couple of years ago, Hedaya was having a rooftop party, and a couple of young guys climbed over the wall. They were both hammered and thought it would be fun. But they changed their minds in a hurry when Bugsy decided he wasn't happy about being woken up."

"What happened?"

"The guys ended up cornered and screaming for help," Mercury said, laughing. "I don't think Bugsy would have hurt them. He'd had a big dinner. But they were petrified. When Hedaya found out what they'd done, he banned them from the casino for life."

"And that was the only time anybody other than you or Hedaya has been in there?"

"Pretty much," he said, nodding. "Natalie sometimes takes care of Bugsy when I have the day off. And Hedaya will occasionally bring a couple of people with him when he goes inside. By and large, it's just him and me."

"I think he's finished his dinner," I said, noticing the lizard who had its nose pressed up against the glass.

"Oh, that was just the first course," Mercury said, laughing. "Hold your horses, Bugsy. I'll be there in a minute."

"What does he eat?"

"I like to rotate it," he said. "It's mostly protein. Chicken, turkey, pork. Occasionally I'll add in some eggs mixed with grain. Today is beef tenderloin."

"Nice."

"Yeah, he likes that. But he'll eat pretty much anything as long as it isn't fish. For some reason, he hates the taste of fish."

"My kind of lizard," I said, glancing at Bugsy.

"What?"

"Nothing," I said, then glanced at my watch. "Okay, thanks. It was nice meeting you, Mercury. I need to get downstairs to watch a matinee."

"Tommy Mandolin?" he said, raising an eyebrow.

"Yeah," I said, deflated.

"Brutal," he said, laughing. Then he caught himself and shrugged. "Sorry. I shouldn't say that. I take it you're a fan."

167

"No, I'm not. My mother is."

"Well, have fun with that," he said, reaching for his access card.

I watched him grab another bowl and step back inside the enclosure. The lizard sat on its haunches directly in front of him and resumed catching the chunks of tenderloin his handler was tossing. I headed down the path until it curved around the back of the enclosure and spotted the rocks and tree branch he'd mentioned. I studied it and confirmed he'd been correct. Climbing inside the enclosure would be a bit of a challenge, but well within the realm of possibilities.

I retraced my steps, waved to Mercury on my way back, then crossed the empty rooftop and caught the elevator down to the main floor. I checked the signage and followed the route to what was called the Cabaret Room. I stopped in the doorway and grinned when I realized I didn't have a ticket. The doorman stared at me as I took a few steps to one side to let other late arrivals get past me. I was about to use my lack of a ticket as the basis for what I considered the perfect excuse for not going to the show when the doorman approached.

"You wouldn't happen to be Suzy, would you?"

"I am. How the heck did you know that?"

"Your mother asked me to give you this," he said, handing me my ticket.

"Crap," I whispered.

"Yeah, I hear that a lot," he said, laughing. "Tommy's show isn't for everyone."

"You mean for people under the age of a hundred?" I said, grinning at him.

"You'll be fine," he said, taking the ticket back for a moment to tear off the bottom section. "And look at that. You're sitting in the front row."

"That's what I was afraid of," I said, giving him a wave as I headed inside and walked down the aisle.

"Tommy's gonna love your shoes," he called after me.

I frowned at the comment but kept walking.

The Cabaret Room looked like it held about a hundred people and it was a plush, intimate setting. I found the gang in the front row, dead center of the stage, and took the empty seat between Josie and my mother.

"You made it," Josie said, shaking her head as she handed my mother a ten-dollar bill.

"Thank you, Josie," she said, sliding the bill into her pocket. Then she beamed at me. "I knew you'd be here. Great seats, huh?"

"What happened, Mom? Wouldn't he let you sit on his lap during the show?"

"Funny, darling," she said, staring expectantly at the stage. "This is going to be wonderful."

I glanced at Josie who shrugged. I leaned in front of her to say hi to Chef Claire, Millie, and Jill who all looked like they'd rather be at the dentist. Then the lights went down and I settled

169

into my seat as the curtain rose. An eight-piece band began playing the intro to a song I remembered from my childhood. Moments later, a well-preserved man probably somewhere in his late seventies made his way onto the stage to a big round of applause. I glanced over at my mother who was clapping wildly and shouting; Tommy!

When I saw the look on her face, I chastised myself and dropped my selfish attitude. I made a commitment to myself that I would smile, applaud, and do my utmost best to enjoy the show. Or at least fake it the best I could. But halfway through Tommy Mandolin's second song, a dreary ballad about how he'd lost his mind in San Diego, a blatant rip-off of a popular song about leaving a different body part in a different city, my commitment wavered.

"Do you know how long the show is?" I whispered, leaning over to Josie.

"An hour and a half," she said with a grimace. "Not counting encore and Q&A."

"Crap," I said, then scowled. "He does a Q&A?"

"Shhh," my mother hissed, then smacked my thigh with her hand without taking her eyes off the crooner.

"Sorry, Mom."

"Shut it."

I sat back and did my best to avoid eye contact with the singer who was spending a lot of time ogling the front row. A half hour in, I started to squirm. After an hour, I was rubbing my forehead and looking at my watch every two minutes. Josie noticed what I was doing and stifled a giggle.

"That's only going to make it seem longer," she said, nodding at my watch. "It's like watching the pot while you're waiting for water to boil."

"I'd much rather be doing that," I said, glancing around. "I wonder if anybody here has a pot I could borrow."

Josie laughed. That drew another strong look of rebuke from my mother. Eventually, Tommy Mandolin finished to wild applause, and after an eternity of the crowd clapping and begging for more, he retook the stage for an encore. When the band played the first few bars of his biggest hit, everyone got to their feet to sing along.

"Oh, no," I said, exhaling loudly. "I completely forgot about this song."

"Me too," Josie said, shaking her head. "And it's going to be stuck in my head all night."

She was right. It was one of those catchy pop songs that seemed clever the first time you heard it. But after hearing it constantly on the radio, and in our living room a hundred times, clever turned into cloying. When the chorus started, the entire crowd, still on their feet, joined in.

Eenie, meenie miny, moe.

A big bear bit me on the toe.

Eenie, meenie miny, moe.

I said stop, but he wouldn't let go.

Eenie, meenie, miny, moe.

Now, I wear these shoes, so it don't show.

Eenie, meenie, miny, moe.

On cue, the entire crowd lifted a foot to display their footwear and rotated their ankles.

"You're not singing along, darling."

"I'm too tired to lift my foot," I said, staring at the rotating red pump she had on display. "Hey, those are nice. Are they new?"

"Yes," she said, not taking her eyes off the crooner. "Now, please be quiet. And remember to mind your manners when we get backstage."

"We're going backstage after the show?"

"We are," she said, glancing over to make solid eye contact. "And that is not up for debate."

"Got it," I said, then frowned. "Hedaya organized it, didn't he?"

"He did," she whispered, then resumed singing along with the chorus that seemed to be stuck on an endless loop. "And it's Mr. Mandolin unless Tommy tells you otherwise."

"Sure, sure."

A lengthy Q&A followed the performance, and when my mother asked her sixth question, I finally hit the wall.

"Really, Mom?" I said, staring in disbelief at her. "Do you really care what his favorite TV show is?"

"Shhh," she said, leaning forward to hear the crooner's response.

172

"Well, given my busy schedule, I don't get a chance to watch a lot of television," he said, giving her a coy smile. "But I guess I'd have to say that old movies are my favorite."

"And all of them silent," I whispered.

That got a snort out of Josie and an elbow in the ribs from my mother. Mercifully, that was the last question, and Tommy Mandolin bowed and left the stage to another wild round of applause. My mother herded us backstage where we were introduced to the singer. We spent a few minutes doing our best to make chit-chat, then we headed for a table and munched on fruit and cheese while my mother fawned and laughed with the guy who insisted on being called Tommy. Just call me Tommy, he'd said with a very expensive smile.

"Good cheese," Josie said, working her way through a small handful. "Sadly, it won't be enough to salvage the afternoon."

"That was brutal," I said, reaching for a slice of cantaloupe.

"It was. But you did good," Chef Claire said, nodding at me. "It was important to her that you be there and you sucked it up."

"Yeah, I guess," I said, glancing around and spotting Hedaya making his way toward us.

"How was the show?" he said.

"I think you know how it was, Hedaya," I said, making a face at him. "Nice touch with the backstage passes."

"I thought you'd like that," he said, grinning at me. "Tommy's fans love him. What ones are left, that is."

"He has a permanent residency here?" I said, still having a hard time believing it.

"Yes," Hedaya said, glancing over at the entertainer who was regaling a small group, including my mother, with a story. "I lose a small fortune on his act, but it's okay. He's a part of the old-time Vegas that's worth preserving."

"Preserving would be the word for it," Josie deadpanned as she snuck another look at the aging singer.

"But don't say a word about my losing money on him. It would crush him."

"That's a really nice thing to do, Hedaya," I said, again feeling bad about my attitude.

"Hey, it makes him happy," he said with a small shrug. "Did you have a chance to talk to her about the dogs?"

"I did," I said, nodding.

"When do you have some time to discuss it?"

"I thought you'd never ask," I said, tossing my bag over my shoulder and pointing at the exit.

Chapter 21

I followed Hedaya to his office and took a seat on the couch while he poured two glasses of wine. He handed me one and sat down across from me.

"I don't think it's too early in the evening for a glass of wine, right?" he said, clinking glasses with me.

"Hey, we're in Vegas," I said, taking a sip.

"Exactly. So, you managed to talk with Maria."

"I did," I said, flashing back to my conversation.

"What did she have to say about the dogs?"

"She doesn't want anything to do with them," I said. "She called them goofy."

"Really? They've always seemed like wonderful dogs to me."

"They are," I said. "But she's not a fan of dogs."

"Cats?" Hedaya said, raising an eyebrow.

"Actually, I think Maria is a fan of Maria," I said, shrugging.

"I see," he said. "What else did she have to say?"

"Well, she's not showing any signs of grief. In fact, she couldn't wait to get me out of the house so she could...catch up with one of her visitors."

"She had visitors?"

"She did. But she didn't know I knew they were there. She said it was the housekeeper. They were hiding in Sergei's office."

175

"Do you know who they were?"

"Alexi and Olga," I said, staring at him.

"Really?" Hedaya said, giving that bit of information some serious thought. "So, that's where they disappeared to."

"And none of them had heard the news about Kosiny," I said. "At least they made it sound like they hadn't."

"I assume you were somehow eavesdropping on their conversation?"

"Yeah," I said, shrugging. "It's kinda what I do."

"I'll try to remember that," he said, laughing. "What else did they have to say?"

"Their best guess is that Natalie threw him off the balcony," I said. "Personally, I don't see it. But who knows?"

"No, I doubt if it was Natalie," he said, shaking his head.

"When I mentioned that Kosiny had gone off the balcony, Maria mentioned the twenty-second floor."

"So, she knew what room he was in," Hedaya said, taking another sip of wine.

"Yeah. Which I interpret to mean that she'd either been there before or he'd mentioned it when he was there visiting. It might mean nothing, but I thought it was interesting."

"She wasn't grieving over Sergei?"

"No, she wasn't. Actually, she was more broken up by the news about Kosiny. I think there was definitely something going on between them," I said, still processing my conversation with her. "Do you know Maria?"

176

"No, I don't," Hedaya said. "From what my sources tell me, she arrived in town a few months ago and started seeing Sergei almost immediately."

"Your sources being Natalie?"

"In this case, yes," he said, nodding. "So, she's not grieving about her dead boyfriend, but she was quite likely having an affair with Kosiny, and this afternoon you think she was about to hop into bed with Alexi."

"That's my best guess so far."

"She gets around," he said.

"You think she's a Russian agent?" I said, leaning forward.

"I'd be shocked if she wasn't," he said, rubbing his forehead.

"So, she's sent here to get close to Sergei and find out what he knows. And probably to get her hands on the key."

"Did they mention the key?" Hedaya said, perking up.

"They did. And it was pretty clear they didn't know where it was or what it unlocked or what the actual information was. But I couldn't miss the fact that all three of them definitely wanted to get their hands on it."

"I'm sure they do," he said. "If it turns out my concerns are accurate, whoever manages to turn that information over to the Russian authorities will be considered a national hero. Especially if it ultimately pushes Russia and China closer together."

"What about Sergei?"

"What about him?"

"Do you really think he was working both sides of the fence?"

"Natalie is convinced he was a double agent. I'm not so sure. Sergei always came across as a full-fledged American patriot. He'd been living here for years."

"He could have been playing the long game, right?" I said.

"Sure. Anything is possible," he said, topping off our wine. "But he had such a good life here. This country had been very good to him. And I still can't see him trying to undermine my efforts. We were very good friends and quite close."

"Maybe he didn't know you were involved in the Chinese thing," I said. "Assuming he knew about it."

"Impossible," he said, shaking his head. "Sergei and I had many conversations over the years about democracy and our intense hatred of autocratic regimes."

"Well, if he wasn't playing you," I said, as an idea bubbled to the surface. "There is another possibility."

"What's that?" Hedaya said, paying very close attention.

"That whatever he's got hidden away doesn't have anything to do with China," I said. "Maybe he had damaging information about Russia."

"That would be wonderful news," Hedaya said, nodding. "But what could it possibly be that would cause someone to kill him?"

"Well, I don't know much about Russian politics," I said, tossing it out. "But there's a certain oligarch who is probably still in bed with a Russian agent who must have several very large skeletons in his closet."

"Alexi," he said, nodding. "I would love it if that's the case."

"A billionaire who made all his money by stealing oil rights. But not until he'd been given permission from the government to do so. The kickbacks he probably has to give the people running the country must be in the millions."

"I'm sure they are," Hedaya said. "But I can't believe that Sergei would just turn over whatever he had to the press. Or our intelligence services."

"Yeah, I get that," I said. "It might not get a lot of traction here, and I imagine the Russians would do everything they could to discredit the story."

"But they must have been getting nervous," Hedaya said. "You know, since they killed him off."

"Maybe Sergei had other motives," I said, staring at the photos on the wall.

"Such as?"

"Blackmail," I said, finally saying out loud the idea that had been floating around my head. "Maybe he was putting the squeeze on Alexi. He can certainly afford to pay it."

"Indeed," Hedaya said. "But why would they kill him off before they got their hands on that key?"

"Because Kosiny, as advertised, really was dumber than a box of rocks," I said, grinning at him.

"Kosiny?"

"Think about it," I said, my neurons finally firing on all cylinders. "Alexi somehow knew that Sergei carried the key with him. So, he had Kosiny take care of him with instructions to grab the key in the process."

"But it's pretty clear that he didn't take care of the situation at all," Hedaya said. "In fact, it's quite possible Kosiny made it worse."

"Hence the decision to toss him off the balcony," I said, raising an eyebrow at him.

"Touché," Hedaya said with a small nod. "But who threw him off?"

"My best guess at the moment is Olga."

"But you said she was surprised to hear the news about Kosiny," he said, frowning at me.

"Well, since they spend all their time lying to other people, I doubt if they have any compunctions about lying to each other.

"Fair point," he said, nodding. "Kosiny killed Sergei? I'm going to need to think about that. It sounds like a stretch."

"Not really," I said, shaking my head. "He could have slipped a slow-acting poison into his drink or dinner. And after we finished eating, everyone started mingling and hanging out around the pool. Kosiny could have easily told Sergei he wanted to have a quiet word with him and they ended up in the rainforest."

"Okay," he said, motioning for me to continue.

"I talked with Mercury today when he was feeding Bugsy," I said.

"Tenderloin day," Hedaya said, laughing. "It's his favorite."

"He was definitely a happy lizard," I said, grinning at the memory of Bugsy snatching chunks of meat out of the air. "Mercury mentioned that you had a problem one time when a couple of your guests climbed over the back wall of the enclosure. I took a look at it, and it's definitely possible to scale the wall."

"Former guests," Hedaya said, scowling.

"My guess is that Sergei was starting to get groggy from the poison. Kosiny was a strong guy and managed to get him in the air and drop him over the glass. Sergei must have been able to get to his feet and walk around a bit until he collapsed in the spot where we found him."

"Why would Kosiny throw him over the wall?" Hedaya said.

"Maybe he thought people would think Sergei had somehow wandered into the enclosure and Bugsy killed him," I said. "Everyone says the guy was a total idiot."

"He was," he said, nodding. "I suppose it's plausible."

"And then Kosiny spotted the key on the ground and realized he'd screwed up. So, he climbed over the glass to get it. He probably panicked the first time he laid eyes on Bugsy. I know I did. And before he could get to the key, Bugsy ate it. We showed up right around that time. Josie mentioned that she heard some rustling in the bushes while she was doing the surgery. Kosiny probably figured that, since you had three of your security guys there, it was going to be impossible for him to get it back."

181

"Kosiny must have known I had the key," Hedaya said, nodding in agreement.

"Yeah, I'm sure he managed to put that together," I said. "So, he went back over the glass on the far wall knowing Sergei was dead and you now had the key. But here's the kicker. Kosiny didn't tell anybody about the key."

"Because he wanted to be the national hero, right?"

"Yeah. Either that or he was thinking about a way to get his hands on a serious chunk of change," I said. "But he went off the balcony before he could figure out a way to get the key from you."

"That's not a bad theory, Suzy."

"Thanks," I said, beaming at him.

"There are still a couple of questions that need to be answered," Hedaya said.

"I know," I said, nodding.

"I imagine that Maria and the rest of them have been all through Sergei's house looking for a safe or some sort of repository."

"I'm sure they have," I said, grinning. "And they can look all they want, but they're not going to find it there."

"You're telling me you know where it is?" Hedaya said.

"I have a pretty good idea," I said. "And I'd be willing to bet that it's right downstairs."

"Moscow Nights?"

"From what I saw, the place is gorgeous," I said. "And the last thing that vodka bar needed was a renovation."

182

"Somewhere in the tasting room?"

"That would be my guess," I said, nodding. "The guy handling the renovation. I think his name is Mika."

"Yes, that's him," Hedaya said.

"Does he work for you?"

"No, Sergei hired him," he said, getting up and heading for his desk. He spoke briefly on the phone then sat back down. "I just asked my head of security to do a little digging into Mika's background."

"When I overheard him talking, he was in the bar with Natalie," I said. "But it might have just been a coincidence."

"I don't believe in coincidences," Hedaya said, shaking his head. "Natalie. I'll need to think about that."

"Which leaves us, for the moment, with only one other unanswered question," I said.

"Who was it that poisoned Sergei?"

"You're sharp as a tack, Hedaya," I said with a grin. "You got any guesses?"

"Apart from Kosiny, no one comes to mind," he said.

"Me either. It had to be Kosiny."

"Look, Suzy. I hate to ask this, but would it be possible for you to stick around a few extra days?"

"No, I'm sorry, Hedaya. I have a wedding to get ready for, and I miss my fiancé and the dogs," I said, shrugging.

"Fair enough. Then I guess there's only one thing I can do," he said, leaning back in his chair.

183

"What's that?"

"Throw another dinner party tomorrow night," he said. "You will be able to make it, won't you?"

"I wouldn't miss it for the world," I said, then remembered. "But we'll need to be out of there by ten or eleven at the latest."

"Why?"

"Girls' night out," I said. "It's our last night here."

"What do you have planned?"

"I don't know," I said, shrugging. "It's supposed to be some big surprise. But I imagine it will include some clubbing, probably a bunch of exotic male dancers, and a lot of drinking."

"When in Rome, right?"

"Whatever it is, it has to be better than the matinee."

"Maybe I can convince Tommy to do a special show for you wearing a G-string," he said, roaring with laughter.

"Don't give her any ideas, Hedaya."

Chapter 22

I headed upstairs to shower and get ready for dinner. Tonight, we were going Italian, and I ran hot water through my hair while various appetizer and entrée combinations ran through my head. Deciding that I should probably wait until I actually saw a menu, I focused on my theories about the dead owner of the vodka bar and what sort of information he'd had that might be worth killing him over.

The idea that Sergei was blackmailing the thieving oligarch continued to resonate with me. If Sergei had damaging information on Alexi, along with a plan to have the information released should anything bad happen to him, it seemed plausible that he would have been able to keep bleeding the billionaire for a long time. That was obviously a dangerous game to play with someone with very close ties to the Kremlin, now evidenced by the fact that Sergei had been murdered.

I vigorously toweled my hair then paused when I felt the all-too-common itch produced by something lurking in my neurons that wasn't ready to make its presence known. I slipped into my robe, draped the towel over my shoulders and walked across the living room onto the balcony. I took a quick peek over the edge and shuddered when an image of Kosiny setting a world record for somersaults on his way down with no one to catch him flashed inside my head. I sat down and tried to get a handle on what was bothering me about my theory.

The idea that it was Kosiny who had tossed Sergei into the lizard's enclosure seemed solid. The aerialist certainly had the opportunity. And the possibility of getting his hands on the information or a lot of money seemed like more than enough motive. The fact that he had screwed up obtaining the key could have been, from his perspective, only a temporary setback.

I was less certain that it had been Olga who had thrown Kosiny off the balcony. But the only other possibility I could come up with was that it was someone else Alexi had sent to do his bidding. And if Olga wasn't working directly with the oligarch, the person who had tossed the aerialist to his death was possibly an individual I had not yet met. That could be a problem for me, and I made a mental note to be on high-alert the rest of the time I was here. Just in case my well-honed sense of snooping wasn't appreciated in Russian circles.

I was more convinced I had a good take on Maria. She'd been sent to Vegas by her handlers to get close to Sergei. And if it was Alexi who was being blackmailed, I was positive she was working directly for the oil thief. If their relationship extended past work into personal, then her dalliance with Kosiny, something I was positive about, had probably emerged out of Kosiny and Maria's regular interactions with each other. As such, their affair might not have been part of the overall strategy to recover the key. I doubted if Maria had shared the fact she'd been sleeping with the aerialist with Alexi, but even if she had, I wasn't sure jealousy was enough of a motive for the billionaire to have him tossed off his balcony. The more I thought about it, the swan dive the aerialist had taken was payback for how badly Kosiny had screwed up trying to recover the key.

I replayed the conversation I had eavesdropped on at Sergei's house. It had been impossible to miss the intensity and frustration in all three of their voices about their inability to locate the missing key. Finding the key remained top of mind for all of them and it had sounded like getting their hands on it was the only thing that mattered. It was as if it were the missing link that, when recovered, would put an end to all their concerns.

And then the missing piece that had been eluding me floated to the surface and smacked me right in the frontal lobe. I stared out at the desert landscape that stretched far beyond the neon lights of the Strip and nodded.

"Duh," I whispered to myself.

The reason their entire focus was on recovering the key was because they already knew the location of where the hidden information was being stored. And as soon as they had figured that out, killing Sergei had been an easy choice, as long as the key was recovered in the process. At the moment, their problems were even worse. Before his death, they had at least known where the key was. Now, they didn't have a clue.

I headed inside where Josie and Chef Claire, also freshly showered and dressed for dinner, were sitting on a couch chatting.

187

"Hey," I said, reaching for my phone.

"Dressing up for dinner I see," Josie deadpanned.

"Funny," I said, making a face at her. "How long have we got before we need to leave?"

"About twenty minutes."

"Plenty of time," I said, nodding as I headed back out to the balcony. I placed the call and waited. "Hi, this is Suzy Chandler. Could I please speak to Hedaya?"

I snuck a quick peek down at the ground, then shuddered again at the prospect of falling from this height. I stepped away from the railing and sat back down on the edge of the lounge chair.

"Hi, Suzy," Hedaya said. "I thought you were heading out to dinner. *Roma*, right?"

"Yeah, that's the place," I said.

"Have the lobster ravioli," he said. "You won't regret it."

"Thanks," I said. "You got a minute?"

"I'm on the phone, aren't I?" he deadpanned.

"You're a funny guy, Hedaya," I said. "I just had an idea."

"About our problem?"

"Yeah," I said, brushing my hair back from my face. "I was replaying the conversation I overheard at Sergei's place earlier."

"Okay," Hedaya said with a touch of confusion in his voice.

"And I remembered that the only thing they talked about was the key."

"Isn't that what you'd expect them to be talking about?" he said, now sounding even more confused.

188

"It is," I said, holding the phone close to my mouth. "As long as they already know the location of where the information is being kept."

Hedaya fell silent for several moments.

"Son of a gun," he whispered. "They know where it's being kept and the only thing they need is the key to put whatever this is behind them." He fell silent again. "Well done, Suzy."

"Thanks. But why haven't they just strong-armed their way inside the thing?" I said, tossing out the question that had surfaced and was beginning to nag.

"Maybe they just learned about the location and haven't had time," Hedaya said. "Or they're worried that the police and others will start looking hard when they discover it was broken into."

"I guess that makes sense. But they'll have to make a move soon, right?" I said.

"Yes. I'm sure they're already making plans to do just that."

"Have you found anything out about Mika yet?"

"My head of security just called from Mika's office," Hedaya said. "And it doesn't look like there's any sort of safe or a secret compartment in the vodka bar. The guy swears up and down that Sergei never asked him to do anything like that."

"And you believe him?" I said, raising an eyebrow.

"You've met my head of security, right?" Hedaya said.

"Charlie? Big bald guy? Used to be a linebacker in the NFL?"

"That's the one," he said.

"What about it?"

189

"Would you lie to him?"

"Good point," I said, knowing that the last thing I, or most people, would do is lie to a chiseled three-hundred-pound guy with a reputation for turning opposing players into tap dancers and game-face stares into wide-eyed, sideways glances when they heard him coming. "Man, I was sure it had to be downstairs in the vodka bar." Then another possibility floated to the surface. "Did Sergei have any other businesses?"

"I believe he was a silent partner in a few other ventures," Hedaya said. "But Sergei never talked much about them. I always assumed they were businesses that were a bit more..."

"Illegal?"

"A rather relative term in this city but, sure, let's go with illegal," Hedaya said, laughing. "Are you thinking that's where the missing information might be located?"

"I am," I said, rubbing my forehead as another idea surfaced.

"And you'd like to find out where Sergei's other businesses might be located?" he said.

"I would."

"Do you have a plan for that?"

"Well, plan might be a bit of a stretch," I said. "At the moment, it's more of a notion."

"I see," he said, chuckling. "Then tell me all about your notion."

"I think we should get into the blackmail business, Hedaya," I whispered.

190

He fell silent for a long time. I waited it out by taking another long look out at the desert.

"That's a very interesting idea, Suzy," he said.

"Yeah, I thought you might like it," I said, grinning. "You wouldn't happen to have a phone number for Alexi, would you?"

"Yes, I do," Hedaya said. "You're convinced Alexi was Sergei's target?"

"Not completely," I said. "And if we start with him and whiff, we'll just regroup and make an offer to the next most logical person. But I'm almost positive it has to be him because he has the most money and potentially the most to lose. Especially if he's been playing footsy with the CIA. And if Alexi takes the bait, we're in."

"I like it," Hedaya said. "But I can't make the call. He knows my voice."

"No, it should be a woman," I said. "You know, posing as one of Sergei's conquests."

"Alexi knows Natalie as well," Hedaya said. "And I really can't involve anyone else who works for me here at the casino."

"I'll do it," I said.

"You? Are you sure?"

"Why not?"

"Well, apart from several felonies you could probably be charged with, I guess not much," Hedaya said, still chuckling but not as vigorously as before. "You got a pen?"

191

"Hang on," I said, heading inside for pen and paper. I ignored the looks Josie and Chef Claire were giving me and returned to the balcony. "Go ahead."

I wrote down the number, read it back to him to make sure I'd gotten it right, then slid the slip of paper into my robe.

"How should we do it?" Hedaya said.

"How good is the driver I was with today at following people?" I said.

"He's very good. The best I've got."

"I thought that you might send him out to Sergei's place," I said. "There's a good chance Alexi's still there with Maria. I'll give him a call and then your driver can follow him."

"Follow him where?" Hedaya said, obviously confused.

"To the place where whatever that key opens is located," I said.

"So, my driver follows Alexi after you make the call and lets me know where the place is," he said. "I like it."

"And then all you'll need to do is figure out a way to get into the place and retrieve it," I said. "You'll probably want to take a small army with you when you go."

"Yes, I imagine I will. And I'll need some time to figure out the best way to do that," he said, sounding concerned about that prospect. "But what if he doesn't take the bait? You know, if he doesn't have a clue about what you're talking about, what then?"

"Like I said, then we'll regroup and come up with another possibility," I said.

"And if we don't get any of the Russians to take the bait?"

"Then you'll need to start worrying about yourself and the future of the Chinese Democratic Front."

"I'd hardly be starting," Hedaya said. "It's been keeping me up most nights. How much should we ask for?"

"That's a good question," I said. "What do you think?"

"Are you thinking about asking for an ongoing amount or a one-shot deal?"

"Probably a one-shot offer," I said, after giving it some thought. "We want him thinking that this is his chance to put the problem behind him once and for all."

"I like it," Hedaya said. "Then you should definitely ask for a big number."

"Twenty million?"

"No, bigger. I'd ask for fifty," Hedaya said. "If the information is as damaging as we think it might be, we should go big."

"Okay," I said, getting ready to end the call since Josie was glaring at me and tapping her watch. "I'll let you know as soon as I speak with him."

"Don't use your own phone," Hedaya said. "Swing by my office. I have several burner phones. Use one of those."

"Got it," I said. "Fifty million it is."

"And you might want to tack on another half a million for me," Hedaya said, again sounding cranky.

"Why would I do that?"

193

"Because your mother took another quarter million off me this afternoon."

Chapter 23

I held up five fingers to Josie and Chef Claire as I headed for my bedroom to throw on a sundress and sandals. I quickly applied a touch of lipstick then added a layer of concealer to the freezer burn on the side of my face that was hanging on a lot longer than I'd expected. I nodded into the mirror then tied my hair back in a ponytail. I walked back into the living room just as my mother and Millie and Jill arrived at our suite.

"It's about time," I said, glancing at my mother. "We've been waiting forever."

"Nice try, darling," my mother said, obviously still basking in the glow of her ongoing luck at the craps table. "Hedaya just called and said our limo is waiting downstairs."

"Let's go," Josie said, grabbing her bag. "I'm starving."

"How are the dogs?" I said to Millie who had appointed herself as their primary caretaker.

"They're great," Millie said, beaming. "They've eaten and been out to take care of business. They have lots of water, and when I left, they were sleeping on my bed in air-conditioned comfort."

I smiled at her and shook my head.

"You want the dogs, don't you?"

"I do," Millie said. "You don't mind, do you?"

"No," I said, glancing at Josie. "We don't mind at all."

195

"They're such great dogs," she said.

"Yeah, yeah, the dogs are great, you're gonna be the perfect mom, and you'll all live happily after," Josie said, ushering everyone to the door. "Let's go. We're gonna be late."

"She's such a delight to be around when she's hungry," I said to Chef Claire.

"Tell me about it," Chef Claire said as she followed me out the door. "I spent the last half-hour trying to keep the key to the mini-bar away from her."

"The key," I said, nodding. "Thanks for reminding me."

"What?" Chef Claire said.

"I need to swing by Hedaya's office on the way out," I said, walking next to her down the hall toward the elevators.

"To pick up a key?" she said, frowning at me.

"No. A phone."

"Should I even ask?" Chef Claire said.

"Probably not," I said, smiling at my mother who was eavesdropping on our conversation. "You won a quarter million after the matinee?"

"I did," she said, beaming back at me. "Since I'm playing with house money, I figured what the heck, right?"

"How much are you up, Mom?"

"About half a million."

"Unbelievable," I said, shaking my head for probably the millionth time at my mother's charmed life.

"What are you going to do with it, Mrs. C?" Jill said, still ebullient about the fact she was up about fifteen thousand.

"Try to turn it into a million, what else?" my mother said, shrugging.

"Got it," I said. "Fifty-one million it is."

"What's that, darling?"

"Nothing."

When the elevator came to a stop on the first floor, I made a beeline for Hedaya's office and tossed the burner phone in my bag. After promising to call him as soon as I'd spoken with Alexi, I walked outside to the limo and climbed in. I ignored the dirty look Josie was giving me and sat quietly during the short ride to the restaurant. Once seated, I studied the menu, decided that the lobster ravioli sounded too fishy, and ordered the pork tenderloin with a side of pasta and the house salad. I grabbed a piece of bread, dredged it in olive oil, then sat back when the sommelier arrived to pour our wine. I took a sip, then excused myself from the table. I headed for the bar, found a quiet corner near the back, draped a napkin over the mouthpiece and made the call.

"Yeah," a sleepy voice said.

"Alexi," I said.

"Yeah? Who's this?"

"I'm the answer to your prayers," I said, keeping my voice low.

"I'm not much for religion," he snapped. "Who is this?"

"I'm someone who holds the *key* to your future."

197

"The key to my future?" he said, still sounding like he'd just woken up.

"Yes. The key."

"I see," he said, now wide awake. "You have the key, do you?"

"I do," I said. "Sergei was kind enough to give it to me for safekeeping before his tragic demise."

"Who are you?"

"Does it matter?" I said, nodding to myself at what I thought was a pretty good question.

"Maybe. Maybe not," Alexi said. Then he fell silent for several moments before continuing. "And you would like to offer this key to me?"

"Very much so," I said. "I certainly have no need for the information. In fact, I have no interest at all in what it actually is."

"I'm glad to hear that," Alexi said. "But while you aren't interested in the information, you are interested in money."

"Nothing gets past you," I said, then flinched. Probably not the best thing to say given my propensity to overuse the line.

"So, I assume your plan is like Sergei's?"

Bingo.

Bait taken. Hook set. Now to slowly reel him in without losing him.

"No, my approach is quite different," I said, deciding to roll the dice. "While Sergei was more interested in an ongoing

198

arrangement, I would much prefer to get this wrapped up in one transaction."

"You would, would you? Hang on a sec. Let me find something to write with," he said, stalling for time. "Keep talking."

"Nice try, Alexi," I said, laughing at him. "You won't have to write it down. And don't bother trying to trace the call. I'm on a throwaway."

"Okay," he said. "Then I won't worry about that."

"You know, Alexi, I can only imagine how much stress this situation has been putting on you," I said.

"Why is that?"

"Well, since you had Kosiny get rid of Sergei the other night, and then Kosiny took that nasty header off his balcony, it's apparent you're starting to show signs of emotional distress."

"That's what I'm doing, huh?" he said, forcing a laugh.

But I knew I'd touched a nerve.

"But again, I have no interest in those situations whatsoever."

"Because you're only interested in money," he said.

"I am. And I'm offering you the chance to put this entire situation behind you once and for all," I said.

"I see. How much?"

"Fifty million."

I waited for his response to the number I'd tossed out. And I waited a long time.

"Okay," he said eventually.

"Really?" I whispered too close to the phone.

"What?"

"Nothing. So, I take it we have a deal?"

"We do," he said. "How do you want to do it?"

We needed to identify the location as soon as possible, but Hedaya had emphasized that he wanted at least a day to carefully orchestrate the recovery of the information. A partial payment was the best I could come up with on short notice.

"I want two million in cash tonight," I said. "You know, as a good faith gesture."

"Tonight?"

"Yeah, I took a bath on the NBA playoffs and my guy is getting impatient. And I've got a good feeling about the Yankees tomorrow."

"So, you're just another inveterate gambler, huh?"

"Yeah, it's a bit of a problem," I said. "And then the first thing Monday morning, you're going to call me and confirm that the other forty-eight million has been deposited into the offshore bank of my choice. I'll give you the phone number and the bank information later tonight."

"We're going to meet tonight?" he said, sounding surprised.

"No, we're not," I said. "You're going to leave the two million, and after I pick it up, I'll be in touch with the bank information. After I confirm all the money has been delivered per my instructions, I'll leave you the key in the same spot."

"How are you gonna do that?"

200

"You let me worry about that, Alexi," I said.

"If you try to steal fifty million from me and not turn over the key, you do know that you'll be a dead woman, right?"

"I'd expect nothing less, Alexi. But you have my word. All I want is the money so I can get far away from you and the rest of my former compatriots. And then you and your *comrades* can get back to looting what's left of the Russian treasury."

"So, you are Russian," he said. "I should have known."

"Let's say I was someone who was close to Sergei and leave it at that."

"Where am I supposed to deliver the two million?"

"To the place where the information is located, where else?"

"That place is going to be filled with drunks tonight," he said.

Bingo.

Sergei owned another bar. I was on a roll. Maybe I should join my mother at the craps table.

"Just wait until after the place closes," I said. "We'll be watching. Just leave it at the location and then you and your henchman need to make yourself scarce. If you do anything stupid, like trying to intercept the exchange, I'll just take the two million in cash then turn the key over to the police. Or maybe the CIA. Or maybe even to your close friend back in Moscow. You got any suggestions about who might enjoy getting their hands on it the most, Alexi?"

"I got the point," he snapped. "Okay, the place closes at two. I'll make sure the money is there by three at the latest."

"Thank you, Alexi," I chirped. "Pleasure doing business with you."

"I do hope we get a chance to meet sometime down the road," he said. "I'd love to have a nice long chat with you."

"You'll have to catch me first."

"Stranger things have happened."

"Absolutely," I said, nodding "And the stories I could tell you."

I hung up and dialed Hedaya. He answered on the first ring.

"Hey. How did it go?" he said.

"So far, so good. Really good, in fact," I said, checking the layer of concealer in the mirror behind the bar to make sure it was holding up.

"You were right about it being Alexi?" Hedaya said, sounding very relieved.

"There's no doubt about it," I said. "If he could have reached through the phone and grabbed me by the throat, it would have been the highlight of his year."

"That's fantastic," he said, then contained his excitement. "The fact that the information is about him, that is. Not the grabbing you by the throat part."

"Got it. He's going to drop off two million in cash as a goodwill gesture at the spot no later than three. I'm pretty sure it's a bar. Did Sergei ever mention owning another one?"

"He dropped some hints occasionally. But nothing specific," Hedaya said. "There's a dive bar in North Vegas that's popular with folks from Eastern Europe. I wonder if that's it."

"Well, your driver is about to find out," I said. "As soon as he figures out where it is, he might want to call for some backup just in case Alexi decides to do something stupid."

"I've already taken care of that," Hedaya said.

"Good. I'll track you down when we get back to the casino after dinner. By the way, my mother is going to try to win another half a million off you."

"Wonderful," he said flatly. "What do you want me to do with the two million?"

"Keep it," I said, laughing. "It'll help you offset your losses."

"I might just do that," he said, laughing along.

"I'll talk to you later," I said, ending the call.

I headed for the bathroom. As soon as I confirmed it was empty, I ripped the back of the phone off and tossed it into a trashcan. I tossed the rest of the phone into the recycling bin next to the bar on my way back to my seat. I sat down and glanced around.

"You were gone awhile," Josie said, looking up from her salad. "Are you feeling okay?"

"I feel fantastic," I said, picking up my salad fork and spearing a tomato wedge.

Chapter 24

For the first time since we'd checked in, I found myself standing in the middle of the casino floor. I glanced around and shook my head at the number of people intensely focused on either trying to win money or doing everything they could not to lose the rest of what they had. To me, it was a strange sight watching the gamblers and their reactions to the non-stop action that had a rhythm all its own. My mother, trailed by Millie and Jill, headed straight for the craps table while Josie and I found a quiet lounge off the main area. We settled around a video poker game designed to look like a coffee table and ordered drinks, which were free as long as we kept feeding the machines. Moments later, Chef Claire and Louie joined us.

"We walked past your mother on the way," Chef Claire said, laughing and shaking her head in disbelief. "A couple of people at the craps table recognized her and bowed out of respect."

"She has to be cheating, right?" I said, hearing my machine make a jangling noise when I hit three of a kind. "How are you doing, Louie?"

"I'm good," he said, glancing around the lounge. "Just trying to figure out what to serve you guys tomorrow night. Hedaya kind of sprung the dinner party on me at the last moment."

"You want some help?" Chef Claire said. "It might be fun to cook together again."

"I think that's a great idea," Josie said, not looking up from her machine. "Dang it. I got nothing. That's five in a row. I think this one is broken."

"Yeah, I'm sure that's the problem," I said, then spotted Natalie talking with someone not far away. "Go ahead and play my machine. I'll be right back."

I headed for the dour spy and she immediately spotted me walking her way. She excused herself from her conversation and met me halfway. She nodded and I followed her to a sitting area. We settled into our seats and she gave me an intense stare that made me uncomfortable.

"Have you talked to Hedaya?" I said, taking a sip of my Limoncello.

"I have," she said. "He said it looks like the information we're looking for deals with Alexi."

"Yes, I'm pretty sure it does," I said. "That should make you feel better."

"It does," she said, nodding through a blank stare.

If she was feeling better about the news, she was doing a great job hiding it.

"How well do you know Alexi?"

"Well enough," she said. "I make it a point to know all the Russians in Vegas." Then she picked up something in the look I was giving her and cocked her head at me. "What is it?"

"I was just wondering how it makes you feel that all those people think you're totally washed up," I said. "You know, as someone who is way past her prime."

"It makes me feel...safe," she said eventually with a shrug.

"Interesting," I said, surprised by her response. "I guess that makes sense. But on an emotional level, how do you deal with it?"

"Pretty much like I deal with everything else," she said, lighting a cigarette. "I'm trained not to let my emotions have much control over what I do."

"Still, it must be hard at times," I said.

"To be considered as basically a dancing bear?" she said, letting loose with what I thought might be a laugh. Then she scowled and her voice began to rise as she started talking. "To be someone who people point their finger at and whisper things into their friend's ear they think I can't hear? To hear people laughing behind my back and completely ignoring all my accomplishments? To consider me a hapless pawn who is no more than a curiosity Hedaya likes to keep around like a pet?"

"Yeah, close enough," I said, leaning back in my chair as she ranted.

"It doesn't bother me," she said, gnawing on her bottom lip.

"Thanks for clearing that up," I said, frowning. "What do you think Alexi is going to do?"

"You mean apart from trying to hunt you down like a dog?"

"He won't figure out it's me," I said.

206

"Well, for your sake, I certainly hope not," she said, exhaling smoke up at the ceiling.

The nonchalant way she said it got my attention and I swallowed hard.

"But Alexi's response will depend on what exactly that information is," she said. "He may decide that it is nothing to worry about and do nothing. He may panic and hop on the first plane back to Moscow and try to plead his case. Or he may hunker down here in Vegas and spend all his time trying to hunt down the people blackmailing him. Just like he did with Sergei."

"Are you worried about what might happen to Hedaya?"

"I worry about Hedaya all the time," she said, shrugging again. "That's my job. But in this case, Hedaya will be just fine."

"I think I might have put his driver in some jeopardy," I said. "He could be walking into a trap later on."

"No, he will be well protected," Natalie said, extinguishing her cigarette.

"You're going to be there?"

"Yes, I am," she said, getting to her feet. "And Alexi is very smart. He will turn over the money tonight and see if he can figure out who's behind it. Two million is pocket change to a man like Alexi. But handing over another forty-eight million is something else altogether."

"But if he sees Hedaya's driver, won't he be able to put it together?"

"If Alexi was around to watch, yes," Natalie said, a small smile appearing briefly. "But it's my job to make sure that he leaves before he gets that chance."

"How are you going to do that?"

"It's amazing what the arrival of several police cars with their sirens blaring does to one's curiosity."

"You're going to call the cops?" I said, nodding. "Nice touch."

"Yes, Hedaya is quite brilliant," Natalie said. "And he has a lot of friends who owe him favors."

"The cops owe him?"

"Can you think of someone better owing you favors?" she said. "Don't worry, as soon as we get the location, it will be handled." She started to walk away then stopped and turned back. "And thank you for your help. You've done very well."

"Thanks," I said, beaming at her.

"Now I understand your interest in espionage," she said, standing close to me. "You probably could have had a career in it. But one word of advice."

"What's that?"

"As soon as this plays out, go home to your dogs," she said with a hard stare that got another swallow out of me.

"That's my plan," I said, nodding. "Can I ask you a question, Natalie?"

"If you must."

"You lead a lonely life, don't you?"

She gave it some serious thought then nodded.

"Yes, I suppose I do."

"Are you coming to dinner tomorrow night?"

"I am," she said. "Why do you ask?"

"Well, after dinner, we're all going out clubbing and who knows what else. Would you like to join us?"

She thought hard again.

"That sounds like it might be a good time," she said, flashing me a genuine smile and waving goodbye as she wheeled around and headed back into the throng of gamblers.

"Male strippers and spies," I said, shrugging as I got to my feet. "Could be fun."

Chapter 25

Saturday

The next morning all six of us decided that a trip to the pool again sounded like a great way to start the day. It was only nine but already hot and getting hotter by the minute as the sun worked its way above the horizon. Including us, there were only a handful of people lounging around the massive pool. I put my lounge chair in an upright position and settled in to start working on my coffee and muffin. Millie and Jill were playing with the spaniels under the cabana and chatting about their continued good fortune at the craps table. Josie and my mother were stretched out in the chairs on either side of me, and all three of us watched Chef Claire effortlessly churn laps.

"She makes it look so easy," my mother said.

"She certainly does," I said, watching as Chef Claire executed a perfect turn at the far end of the pool and began freestyling her way back.

"It may look easy," Josie said, glancing up from the magazine she was reading. "But it's a lot of work. I get tired just watching her."

"You're right," I said, nodding. Then I glanced over at her and grinned. "I'm gonna count it."

210

"I'd be shocked if you didn't," Josie said, then went back to her magazine.

"How did you do last night, Mom?"

"Oh, let's not talk about it," she said, waving it off.

"You lost?"

"Of course not," she said, lowering her sunglasses to make eye contact. "I just don't like to gloat."

"She lost," I said, glancing over at Josie. "Did you check in this morning with Sammy?"

"I did," she said. "Two new drop-offs yesterday. A couple of Labs were found roaming along the side of Route 12. But Sammy is pretty sure he knows who they belong to. And we had an adoption."

"That's great. Which dog?"

"The short-haired Terrier," Josie said. "Sophia Jensen swung by the Inn to take a look at the dogs, and she flipped over Willy as soon as she saw him. They'll be very happy together."

"Perfect match," I said, nodding. "Did the guys play poker again?"

"They did. And Sammy swears they kept their cigars on the porch," Josie said, then glanced at the edge of the pool when Chef Claire climbed out right in front of us.

"How many laps did you do?" I said, watching as she removed her earplugs and goggles and toweled off.

"Only thirty," she said, breathing heavily as she sprawled out on the lounger next to Josie.

211

"Slacker," Josie said, going back to her magazine.

Chef Claire playfully snapped her towel at her then drained half a bottle of water.

"So, how's Louie?" I deadpanned.

"Don't start, darling. I think he's a lovely young man."

"Yeah, he is," Chef Claire said. "But he's changed since culinary school."

"How so?" I said, glancing over at her.

"Well, in cooking school, he was always so playful. And nothing ever seemed to bother him. Now, he seems more serious. You know, like he's somehow carrying the weight of the world on his shoulders."

"Age will do that to you," my mother said. "Not a word, young lady."

"Geez, Mom. You take all the fun out of it," I said, laughing. "What makes you say that?"

"It's hard to explain," Chef Claire said. "Louie just seems different."

"I noticed it hasn't seemed to slow you down," Josie said, grinning at her. "Do you see a future with this guy?"

"Probably not past tomorrow afternoon," Chef Claire said, shrugging. "But we'll always be good friends."

I glanced out at the pool and spotted Hedaya making his way toward us carrying a briefcase. He beamed at us when he approached and came to a stop directly in front of me.

"Good morning, ladies," he said, glancing around.

212

"You're in a good mood," I said, then nodded at the briefcase. "Is that what I think it is?"

"It is," Hedaya said.

"What is it?" my mother said, immediately suspicious. She glanced back and forth at Hedaya and me and waited.

"Let's call it a windfall," Hedaya said.

"Well, you didn't get it from me," she said, smiling up at him.

"Sadly, no," Hedaya said. "Do you have a minute, Suzy?"

"Sure," I said, climbing out of the lounger and following him to a nearby table. "What's up?"

"I just thought you'd want to know that things went well last night. My driver got the location and we were able to execute the diversion perfectly."

"Natalie mentioned something last night about having the cops show up," I said.

"Apparently, it went off without a hitch," he said, his eyes dancing. "And I must remember to comp the police chief the next time he comes in. When Alexi heard the sirens and saw the lights, Natalie said three cars quickly exited the scene."

"You had the cops raid the bar?"

"No, they were supposedly responding to a disturbance at the used car dealership next door," Hedaya said. "But Alexi didn't know that and decided to hit the road. He must be incredibly nervous about whatever Sergei had on him."

"What's the name of the bar?"

"Evil Ways," Hedaya said. "A total dive bar and the last place anybody would look."

"Did your driver or Natalie get a chance to look around?"

"No, their instructions were to grab the briefcase and get out of there right away," Hedaya said. "Natalie will be checking the place out tonight after they close."

"And grab whatever is in the safe and bring it to you," I said.

"That's the plan," Hedaya said. "And based on the information, we'll decide what to do with it."

"Won't Alexi have people watching the place?"

"I'm sure he will try," he said. "But Natalie is very good at what she does. She mentioned that she is going out with you after dinner."

"She is," I said. "That's okay, right?"

"It's fine. And the perfect cover. It was very kind of you to invite her. I don't think Natalie has a lot of friends. Just don't let her drink too much."

"Geez, Hedaya," I said, grinning at him. "A bachelorette party in Vegas. What are the odds of that happening?"

"Funny. Just don't let her have too many shots of vodka."

Chapter 26

For dinner, Chef Louie decided to serve something he called the Baker's Dozen Trio. According to Hedaya, it was one of his personal chef's go-to menus when the casino owner, as he often did during the summer months, decided to invite several people to dinner on the rooftop on short notice. The baker's dozen reference came, of course, from the idea of a baker throwing in an extra item when a customer ordered a dozen baked treats. The trio referenced the thirteen different proteins throwing off incredible smells from the nearby grill, the various salads sitting in metal bowls on a large bed of ice, and a collection of thirteen different desserts apparently being kept under wraps in the walk-in cooler until needed. Based on the lustful looks all of us were giving the grill and the collection of salads, keeping the desserts out of reach was probably a good call on Louie's part.

"Who was it that said thirteen was an unlucky number?" Josie said, beaming at the grill.

Louie heard her comment and laughed as he expertly flipped a long row of bone-in ribeye steaks that were at least three inches thick then turned his attention to another item I didn't recognize. I glanced around at the invited guests who were casually chatting in pairs and small groups near the pool. Alexi, doing his best to demonstrate he didn't have a care in the world, was chatting with Olga, who'd arrived with a bandage on her ankle and a small limp.

According to her tale of woe, a cover story I was quite sure, she had landed awkwardly during afternoon warmup and had been given the night off from the show. Hedaya was getting acquainted with Maria. At first, she had politely refused his invitation over the phone, but he had eventually convinced her that dinner with friends, both old and new, was a good way to take her mind off the recent tragic events.

My mother and Jill sidled up next to me. I gave both of them hugs then admired my mother's outfit.

"You look great, Mom."

"Thank you, darling," she said, giving me the once-over. "You too. You've outdone yourself."

"Well, I wanted to look nice for the strippers," I deadpanned. "Are you sure you're up for another late night?"

"Yeah, I think I'll be able to handle it," she said, shaking her head at me and checking the name cards that were sitting on the table. Then she focused on me again and made a point of making solid eye contact. "I couldn't help but notice that you and Hedaya have been very chatty the past few days."

"He's a wonderful man," I said, glancing away. "What about it?"

"Oh, I'm just being nosy," she said.

I laughed and looked at Jill.

"Now you know where I get it from."

"Are you up to something, darling?"

"Relax, Mom," I said, waving it off. "I just love listening to Hedaya's stories."

"Uh-huh," she said, then glanced at Jill. "Come on, dear. Let's go sit down. We're sitting with Hedaya and Rose."

I watched them head for their seats then glanced at the seating arrangements. Apart from Sergei, who wouldn't be joining us for obvious reasons, my section of the table was identical to the other night. I was sitting directly across from Alexi. Josie and Chef Claire were again on either side of him and Natalie was on my left. Maria was in Sergei's spot and occupying the seat to my right. Next to her was Olga. We sat down and I glanced around the table. I didn't recognize any of Hedaya's other guests, but it was clear they weren't Russian.

Hedaya welcomed everyone, made a short toast, then informed everyone that dinner was buffet style. On cue, a couple of servers arrived carrying various serving utensils, and a line began to form in front of the salads. I slipped into line behind Josie who kept sneaking glances back and forth from the salads to the grill, obviously developing her game plan.

"What are you going to start with?" she said, glancing over her shoulder.

"Those crab legs look amazing," Chef Claire said.

"I'm sure one of those ribeyes has my name on it," I said, grinning at Louie who was standing nearby manning the grill.

"Just your name?" Josie said, laughing. "They're big enough to add your life history."

"I'll just take the leftovers for Moose and Squirrel," I said, sliding my salads to the edge of my plate to make room for the steak. I pointed at one and Louie placed it on my plate. I felt the weight and shook my head at the size of it.

"Heavy, huh?" Louie said, grinning at me. "You're in for quite a workout getting through that."

"Yeah, I know. I'm gonna count it."

"What?"

"Nothing," I said. "Thanks, Louie. Everything looks fantastic."

"You're very welcome," he said. "So, where's your first stop tonight after dinner?"

"It's someplace called Shot City," I said, with a shrug.

"Hey, how about that?" he said, removing several crab legs from the grill and piling them high on a platter. "It's one of my regular hangouts. After we finish our shifts, a lot of the chefs from around town head over there for a nightcap. Maybe I'll see you guys there later on. I'll swing by and say hi."

"That would be great," I said, then couldn't resist. "I know Chef Claire would love that." Then I flinched when I felt a sharp pain in one of my ankles. "Ow."

"Oh, sorry about that," Chef Claire said, flicking the back of my ear hard with a finger. "I should pay attention to where I'm walking."

I glared at her and rubbed my ear as I limped back to my seat. Natalie and Maria were already working their way through their

218

meal. I slipped in between them and savored my first bite of steak. I turned to my left but caught the slight nod Natalie was giving me, apparently instructing me to chat with Maria first.

"So, how are you holding up?" I said to her.

"Oh, I'll be fine," Maria said, rapidly working her way through what looked like a half-chicken.

"What is that?" I said, realizing it was too big to be chicken.

"Wild pheasant," Maria said. "It's amazing."

"Have you decided if you're going to stay in the house or not?" I said, slicing off another piece of steak.

"Not yet," she said, with an unconcerned shrug. "It's going to depend."

"Sure, sure," I said, deciding not to push the conversation.

I glanced across the table at Alexi who, once again, was regaling Josie and Chef Claire with a story. They were both paying close attention, and I again wondered if I should have brought them up to speed about what Hedaya and I were up to. But Josie and Chef Claire were no threat to the oligarch, and I was sure they'd be completely safe around him, especially given the rooftop setting and the presence of two large security guards standing off to one side near the elevator.

"How's your dinner?" I said to Natalie.

"Incredible," she said. "I might have to get another lobster tail."

"Alexi seems incredibly calm," I whispered, leaning in close to her.

219

"Yes, he does," she said, sneaking a glance at him. "Trust me, he's not."

I glanced down the table at Hedaya who was listening to a conversation my mother and Rose were having. But it was obvious he was more interested in what was happening at our section of the table. I gave him a slight shrug, and he nodded then went back to his dinner.

"Hedaya said not to let you drink too much vodka tonight," I said, chuckling.

"He worries too much," Natalie said, wiping garlic butter off her mouth. "Vodka is like water to me."

"Are you sure you don't want company tonight?" I said.

"No, on missions like this one, I always work alone," she whispered.

"Okay," I said, nodding. "But if you feel like company, just let me know."

"If I feel like company, I'll swing by the pool," she said, giving me a look that ended the conversation.

"Got it," I said, then focused on my garden salad that was highlighted with walnuts and blue cheese.

"So, are you looking forward to being married?" Natalie said, after sneaking another glance across the table at the oligarch who was now listening closely to something Chef Claire was saying.

"Very much so," I said. "Actually, I can't wait."

"What does your fiancé do for work?"

"He's a disaster relief consultant," I said. "He travels all over the world."

"Well, hopefully, he'll be able to cut back and spend more time with you," Natalie said. "Spending time together is very important. Especially early in a marriage."

"We've actually been talking about that," I said. "But he loves his work."

"As do you," she said, taking a sip of wine.

"Absolutely," I said, nodding. Then I sighed audibly when I remembered how much I was missing Max and the dogs.

"Are you okay?"

"I'm fine. But I am looking forward to getting home," I said.

"Yes, I can see it already," Natalie said, lightening up and almost cracking a smile. "A night of debauched revelry followed by the flight home nursing a massive hangover. A classic cliché, am I right?"

"Nothing gets past you," I said, laughing.

Then I paused when I caught the look Alexi was giving me after he heard my comment. It made the hairs on the back of my neck stand up and I did my best not to panic. I dropped my fork on the floor and slid down under the table, ostensibly to retrieve it.

"Natalie," I whispered. "Natalie."

"Do you need some help?" she said, glancing down.

"Yes. Get down here."

"What on earth is the matter with you?" she said, inches away from me under the table.

"I think Alexi just made me," I said, then noticed my hands were shaking when I picked up my fork.

"How on earth did he do that?" she said, stunned.

"I used the same phrase with you as one I used with him on the phone last night."

"What?"

"My comment about how nothing gets past you," I said, frantic. "I said the same thing to Alexi on the phone."

"So, you were trying to be clever, and it's come back to haunt you," she said, shaking her head. "A good spy must remain vigilant in all conversations."

"Don't nitpick. What are we going to do?"

"First, we are going to get back in our seats and finish our dinner," she said.

"And then?"

"I'm sure I'll think of something," she said with a shrug.

"Thanks, that makes me feel so much better," I said, sitting up and realizing a server was standing directly behind me holding out a clean fork. "Oh, thank you. I'm such a klutz." I smoothed my napkin out on my lap and did my best to avoid making eye contact with the oligarch who continued to keep a close eye on me.

"Eat," Natalie whispered without looking at me.

I cut another piece of steak and chewed nervously. I swallowed hard without tasting it and forced down a sip of water. I glanced down the table at Hedaya who had definitely picked up on my distress. I swallowed another bite, took a sip of wine, then wiped my mouth. I continued to hold the napkin up to my mouth.

"What have you got?" I whispered to Natalie.

"I'm thinking," she whispered back.

"Are you okay?" Maria said, glancing over at me.

"Oh, I'm fine," I said. "I think that last piece of steak went down the wrong way."

"Try taking human bites," she said, staring off into the distance with a smug look I so wanted to knock off her face.

Normally, I would have spent some time working on a snappy comeback, but the oligarch continued to give me a narrow-eyed glare from across the table.

"Natalie," I whispered again after coughing into my napkin. "He won't stop staring at me."

"Yes, I noticed," she said casually. She slid the last piece of the lobster tail into her mouth. "You have definitely, as you so eloquently put it, been made."

"I hate when that happens," I said, toying with my salad. "What are we going to do?"

"So, it's we now, is it?" she said, for some reason deciding to go for funny.

I shook my head and forced a smile at her. Then I glanced down the table at Hedaya who was staring back at me with a deep frown. I glanced across the table at Alexi who was paying close attention to something Josie was telling him.

"Natalie. C'mon. Hurry up," I said, my hands shaking gently as I reached for my water glass.

"I think we should go for a walk after dinner," she whispered.

"A walk?"

"Yes."

"A walk where?"

"In the rainforest," she said.

"That's all you got?" I said, staring at her in disbelief.

"Do you have a better idea?"

Good question.

"No," I said. "What are we going to do on the walk?"

"Improvise."

"Thanks for clearing that up," I said, staring down at my plate.

"I'll think of something," she said. "We'll just start strolling off. I'm sure Alexi will follow."

"Him and his henchmen," I said.

"No, his henchmen aren't here this evening," she said. "The only person we might have to worry about is Olga. She is very strong. And quite vicious when the mood strikes."

"What about Maria?" I whispered.

"No, Maria is not a danger. Her talents lie elsewhere. But I would be willing to bet that Alexi will want to handle this problem by himself."

"Why's that?" I said, sneaking another peek at the oligarch who was still focused on the story Josie was telling him.

"Because you've made it personal," Natalie said with a shrug.

I sat quietly for a long time then nodded.

"Okay, a walk in the rainforest it is," I said, glancing at the servers who were setting out an impressive display of desserts. "You want to have dessert first? It might be the last time we get the chance to eat it."

"There you go with the we again," she said, grinning at me.

"Funny," I said, biting my bottom lip. "But maybe we should wait on dessert."

I saw Hedaya get up from his seat and begin working his way down the table chatting with all his guests. When he was standing behind Natalie, he beamed and glanced back and forth at us.

"Did you enjoy your dinner?" he said, obviously concerned but doing his best not to show it.

"It was wonderful, Hedaya," Natalie said. "But I think that Suzy and I have decided to go for a stroll in the rainforest to walk all this food off before we have dessert."

"That sounds like a good idea," he said, making solid eye contact with the spy. "Maybe I'll join you in a few minutes. I'll *follow* you after I finish chatting with the rest of my guests."

"We'll be looking for you, Hedaya," Natalie said, then took a sip of wine as she sat back in her chair.

225

Hedaya didn't miss a beat as he took a couple of steps to his right to chat with Maria and Olga. Natalie got up from her seat and I followed suit. Most of the guests were huddled around the selection of desserts and not paying attention to us. Except for Alexi. It was pretty clear he was keeping a close eye on what we were doing. But Hedaya was doing a great job keeping Olga and Maria occupied, and I was certain they didn't see us leave the table.

I fought the urge to run to the rainforest until Natalie placed a hand on my arm to slow me down.

"We're just two people enjoying a casual stroll after dinner," she said as we made our way past the massive pool.

"That's easy for you to say," I said, forcing myself to walk slower. "What are we going to do if he shows up?"

"Oh, he'll show up," she said. "In fact, he's already following us."

"He is? How do you know that?"

"With my super-spy, reverse-vision glasses," she deadpanned, continuing to stare straight ahead.

"What?"

"I'm joking," she said, stifling a laugh. "I caught his reflection in the pool."

"How can you stay so calm?"

"It's time like this when remaining calm is essential," she said, finally making eye contact.

"Yeah, I really need to start working on that."

226

"No, what you should do is focus on your fiancé and your dogs," she said, veering left as we approached the entrance to the rainforest. "Let's go say hello to Bugsy."

I let the idea marinate for a few seconds then nodded.

"Hey, that's good."

"Yes, I thought so, too."

Chapter 27

We entered the rainforest, and Natalie again placed a hand on my arm to keep my pace to a leisurely stroll. I forced myself to keep breathing, and the sounds of the birds and the sight of the stars shining through the glass ceiling far above did help me relax a bit. But it was hard to keep from glancing back to try and get a bead on the oligarch Natalie was certain was following us.

"What's the plan?" I said as we approached the enormous glass enclosure.

"We pick a spot and wait."

"A hiding place," I said, nodding. "Good call."

"No, we're going to stand right out in the open."

"Okay," I said, glancing into the enclosure as we strolled along the teak path. "Probably wouldn't have been my first choice, but you're the professional."

"You know," she said casually as we continued walking. "This reminds of another mission I was on several years ago in the Brazilian jungle."

"Really? How did that one go?"

"Not well," she said with a shrug.

We came to a stop next to the door that led into Bugsy's lush surroundings. I rocked back and forth on my heels and did my best to look casual.

"So, this is the spot, huh?" I said, glancing around.

228

"It is," Natalie said, peering through the glass for signs of the lizard. "I don't see him anywhere."

"No, Bugsy seems to be turned in for the night."

I flinched at the deep voice with the thick Russian accent. I did a half-turn and eventually managed to summon up a small smile.

"Hi, Alexi," I said. "Nice night for a walk, huh?"

"I think you've done all the walking you're going to be doing, Suzy," he said, casually removing a large handgun from behind his back and pointing it at us. "Unless you want to count the walk to the elevator."

"Elevator?" I said, frowning.

"Yes. The elevator that will take us down to the lobby and then to my limo that is waiting outside for us."

"Geez, I don't know, Alexi," I said. "It's a nice offer, but I've already made plans for the evening. Bachelorette party, you know."

"I'm afraid your friends will have to ogle and drink by themselves this evening," Alexi said, then focused on Natalie. "I'm a bit surprised that you're involved in this situation, Natalie. Whatever happened to your supposed retirement?"

"I'm not following you, Alexi," Natalie said. "We're just out for an after-dinner stroll."

"Of course," he said. "What's your cut of the fifty million?"

"Fifty million?" Natalie said, frowning. "I have no idea what you're talking about, Alexi."

229

"Would you like to hand over the key now?" he said, again focusing on me. "Or would you like to wait until we reach the shed?"

"The Shed?" I said, gulping. "That wouldn't happen to be the name of a club by any chance?"

"No," he said, laughing. "I doubt if you'll feel much like dancing after you've spent some time in the shed."

I glanced down the pathway but saw no sign of Hedaya. I decided to try and stall for time.

"So, what's the deal, Alexi? Sergei must have had some very damaging information on you if you're willing to cough up fifty million after one phone call," I said.

"You haven't read it?" he said, surprised.

"Like I told you on the phone last night, my only concern is the money. I don't have any interest in what's inside that safe."

"I see," he said, nodding as he gave it some thought. "Interesting."

"Does that make a difference?"

"Sadly, for you, no," he said, waving the pistol at us. "Now, if you don't mind, we should get going. There are a couple of gentlemen waiting downstairs who are just dying to have a chat with you. And you as well, Natalie."

"There you are," a voice called out from down the path. "I should have known I'd find you in here."

Alexi did a half-turn when he heard Hedaya's voice, and Natalie sprang forward. She grabbed Alexi's wrist and bent it back until I heard a loud snap that could have been a tree branch breaking. Unfortunately for Alexi, it wasn't. He dropped the gun and screamed in pain as he clutched at his wrist. Natalie viciously kicked him just below the waist, and Alexi's eyes grew wide, and he dropped to his knees. She leaned down and picked up the gun. The entire sequence couldn't have taken more than five seconds. Natalie checked to make sure the safety was on then slid the gun behind her back and tucked it into her waistband. Then she removed an access card from her pocket, and I heard the door click open.

"Suzy," she said, grabbing the moaning Alexi by the collar. "If you would be so kind to hold the door."

I did, and I watched with an open-mouthed stare as Natalie effortlessly dragged the large man into the enclosure and shoved him hard to the ground. She stepped out of the enclosure and closed the door behind her.

"Are you two okay?" Hedaya said, coming to a stop next to us.

"Yeah, we're fine," I said, still stunned by what I'd just witnessed. "Natalie, that was amazing."

"Thank you," she said without emotion.

Then she glanced at Hedaya and nodded her head at Alexi who had managed to sit up. He continued to grimace and hold his wrist. But judging from the tentative movements he was making as he tried to find a comfortable sitting position, the broken wrist might not have been his biggest problem.

231

"Make the call, Alexi," Hedaya said. "Call your people and tell them that the problem is resolved and they can take the rest of the evening off."

"Why would I do that, Hedaya?" Alexi said, managing defiance despite his situation. "All I need to do is wait. Eventually, they'll come looking for me."

"Okay, have it your way," Hedaya said. Then he whistled softly. Moments later, Bugsy came lumbering out of the shadows and stopped directly in front of Hedaya. "Good boy."

Then Bugsy noticed he had company and he turned around and looked at the interloper with the broken wrist. Alexi groaned as he did his best to scramble away from the giant lizard who continued to give him an inquisitive stare.

"He's much more imposing when you're inside the enclosure with him, wouldn't you say?" Hedaya said, grinning at the oligarch. "Make the call. In English, if you don't mind."

Alexi retrieved his phone from his pocket, made the call, then Natalie opened the enclosure and stepped inside.

"How are you tonight, Bugsy?" she said, grabbing the phone out of Alexi's hand.

"Where did you get the access card?" I said, frowning.

"It's Mercury's day off tomorrow," she said. "I feed Bugsy a couple days a week. Don't I, Bugsy?"

I wouldn't have believed it if I hadn't seen it with my own eyes, but the lizard turned its head to look at Natalie and then thumped its tail like a dog.

"What do you want to do with him, Hedaya?" Natalie said, again focused on the groaning oligarch.

"Let's just leave him here for now," Hedaya said. "Bugsy will keep a close eye on him. After we get our hands on whatever information Sergei had, we'll decide what to do with him."

"You can't leave me in here with this thing, Hedaya," Alexi said, staring in disbelief at the casino owner.

"Why not?"

"Because he's liable to eat me," Alexi said, glancing back and forth at Hedaya and the lizard.

"Don't worry, Alexi," Hedaya said with a big grin. "He's already had his dinner. But try not to draw too much attention to yourself. Sometimes Bugsy does enjoy a late-night snack."

"Hedaya, please."

"You'll be fine, Alexi," Hedaya said. "And don't worry, as soon as we get our hands on the information, you'll be the first to know. Oh, I do hope you're not afraid of the dark."

"What?"

"Bugsy sleeps better in the dark," Hedaya said, then cackled loudly.

He gestured for us to follow him and we headed down the path back toward the rooftop. Alexi continued to call out, pleading his case. Eventually, his voice faded and was replaced by the sound of the waterfalls just outside the entrance to the rainforest.

"Well done, Natalie," Hedaya said. "It's nice to see that your skills are as sharp as ever."

"How do you do that wrist thing?" I said.

"*You* don't," she said, giving me a hard stare.

"You're no fun."

"Okay, I guess we're all set," Hedaya said. "I hope you ladies have a wonderful time tonight. Just wait until the bar closes, Natalie, and then go in and grab whatever is in the safe. You shouldn't have any problems now that Alexi has told his guys to take the night off. And try not to drink too much vodka. You know how you get."

"I'll be fine," Natalie said. "Knowing Alexi's henchmen like I do, they'll be the ones in a vodka haze by midnight."

"I'll be in my office so stop by as soon as you get back to the casino," Hedaya said, then looked at me as we continued to make our way back to where we'd eaten dinner. "Thank you, Suzy. You did some wonderful work, and I'll never forget it."

"My pleasure, Hedaya."

Hedaya came to a stop and waved to the two security guards near the elevator. We waited until they approached then Hedaya glanced back and forth at them.

"Alexi will be spending the evening with Bugsy," Hedaya said and waited until both security guards stopped laughing. "But just to be safe, give Enrique and Wilber a call and have them guard both exits."

"You got it, Hedaya," one of the security guards said. "Anything else?"

"Actually, there is," he said, pointing at Olga and Maria. "I think it might be a good idea for you to escort those two ladies down to the basement."

"The basement?" a guard said, glancing at the other.

"No, nothing like that," Hedaya said, shaking his head. "Just put them in one of the holding cells and keep a close eye on them until I call you."

"You got it, Hedaya."

"And be careful with the bleached blonde. She can be nasty."

Chapter 28

I stared in disbelief at my mother. She was showing off her flexibility by doing the limbo under a pole about three feet above the stage. Each end of the pole was being held by an exotic dancer who apparently got their costume design inspirations from watching Gladiator. They, along with the rest of the crowd at Shot City, cheered wildly when my mother made it under the bar, worked her way upright and, in an impressive demonstration of her ability to *hang with the girls*, did a tequila body shot out of another dancer's navel. I shook my head in disbelief then approached the stage and snapped a couple of close-ups with my camera phone for posterity.

You never know when something like that might come in handy.

I sat back down and shook my head again at my mother who was prowling the stage with her arms raised above her head like a boxer who'd just scored a first-round knockout. And since my mother had just finished her fifth *round*, I didn't like her chances of going the distance. But I had to give her props: She was hanging tough.

I glanced to my left at Chef Claire who was laughing and applauding, then at Millie and Jill across the table who were doing the same. Then one of the bartenders rang a bell behind the bar, and the crowd roared and chanted.

236

Ready or not.

I got shot.

And then the crowd in unison tossed back a shot of their beverage of choice and slammed the shot glass down on the table in front of them. Except for me. I'd stopped a half-hour ago at two drinks. I considered asking our server for a glass of wine but decided against it when I realized I might get booed out of the club. I stared down at my untouched shot of silver Patron then casually slid it over in front of Josie who was sitting to my right. I nudged her elbow, and she paused from the conversation she was having with Natalie to glance at me. Then she looked down at the fresh shot I was pointing at.

"I thought I just drank a shot," Josie said, slurring and gently swaying back and forth in her chair. "Is that mine?"

"It is," I said above the noise.

She leaned in close and whispered.

"Don't let me have too many of these. I have work to do."

"You do?" I said with a grin. "When?"

Josie stared off then shrugged.

"Sometime," she said, tossing back the shot and turning back to Natalie. "So, Natasha, tell me. What's it like to be a spy?"

"It's Natalie."

"Really?" Josie said, glancing around the club. "I'm glad she finally made it."

I glanced at Chef Claire who, while mildly buzzed, was doing a much better job of holding it together.

237

"Having fun?" I said.

"I'm having a blast," Chef Claire said. "How are you doing?"

"I'm good. Just taking a bit of a break from the tequila," I said, then glanced at my mother who was still on stage and twerking with all three dancers. "Unbelievable."

"That's the word for it," Chef Claire said. "She is amazing. You gotta give her that much."

"Yeah, she's pretty special," I said, studying the expression on my mother's face. "But don't you dare tell her I said that."

"Don't worry. Your secret is safe with me," she said, sliding her drink across the table next to the collection of shot glasses in front of Millie and Jill. Then she glanced at my mother again before leaning in close to be heard above the music. "Your mother certainly has a strong will."

"Yeah. But she's got a really weak won't," I said, laughing.

Chef Claire laughed along then paused to look up when she felt a hand on her shoulder.

"Hi, guys," Louie said, glancing around the table.

"Hey, Louie," Chef Claire said. "You want to join us?"

"No, I just stopped by to say hi," he said. "I'm with a few chef buddies on the other side of the bar. And I'm not sure I'm ready for this."

He took another look around the table, nodded and waved to everyone, then focused on my mother who was now leading the crowd in a bad, yet highly energetic, rendition of *Boogie*

238

Wonderland. We watched her for a few moments, then it was Louie's turn to shake his head.

"How does she do that in those stilettos without snapping an ankle?" he said.

"She made a deal with the devil," I deadpanned.

"Look, I need to head back," he said. "But I'll swing by the pool in the morning to say goodbye before you fly out."

"You might want to make it early afternoon," Chef Claire said.

"Got it," he said, grinning at her. "Millie. Jill. Have a wonderful evening." Then he draped an arm over Josie and Natalie's shoulders. "Try not to overdo it."

"That's good advice, Louie," Josie slurred.

"What?" Natalie said, cocking her head.

Louie leaned over and whispered into Natalie's ear. She nodded and raised a finger to let him know she understood. He waved and slowly worked his way through the crowd.

"He's nice," I said to Chef Claire.

"Yes, he is," she said, frowning. "But just a little weird for my tastes."

"Yeah, nobody wants that," I said, staring up at my mother.

The bell rang again and the crowd chanted in unison.

Ready or not.

I got shot.

I watched as everyone at our table tossed back another shot. I glanced at Natalie to make sure she was going to be sober enough to make her way to the dive bar. So far, her reputation as someone who could hold her booze was bearing out, and she smiled at me and raised her empty shot glass at me in salute. Then her eyes rolled back in her head, and she fell forward. Her forehead banged hard on the table, and she remained in that position, passed out.

"Hey, Lightweight," Josie said, nudging Natalie's arm. "Wake up."

But Natalie was down for the count.

"Geez, Natasha," Josie said, staring down at her drinking partner. "You might be a whiz drinking vodka, but you suck at tequila."

"Crap," I whispered.

"What's the matter?" Chef Claire said.

"Nothing," I said, staring at Natalie.

I checked my watch and realized it was almost closing time. Our original plan was to go club hopping, but after the male revue show, we'd decided to stay at Shot City for the limbo contest. Time had gotten away from me, and I calculated we'd been here since eleven, a three-hour onslaught of tequila shots punctuated with Pavlovian chants.

And now, Natalie was officially on the disabled list. I had a few options available, and I was just about to review them and maybe call Hedaya for guidance when my mother began leading a conga line that was soon weaving its way through the tables. She waved at us and my four friends got to their feet.

"Aren't you coming?" Chef Claire said.

240

I came to a decision on the spot and shook my head.

"No, I better stay here and keep an eye on Natalie."

"Okay," Chef Claire said, placing her hands on Millie's shoulders and joining the back of the line.

I got up and sat down next to the unconscious Natalie who was either snoring or mumbling in Russian. I gently tapped the side of her face, and she came too just long enough to swat at my hand.

"I can't believe it," I said, giving my mother a finger wave as she led the long line past our table. "C'mon, Natalie. Wake up."

But Natalie was done. And I knew it. I sat back to ponder the situation then realized that the solution was easy. Since Alexi, along with Olga and Maria, were under Hedaya's supervision and his henchmen had been told to take the rest of the night off, all I needed to do was head out to Evil Ways and retrieve the information by myself. I concentrated and finally remembered the access code Hedaya had mentioned earlier. According to Natalie, punching the code into the keypad outside the back entrance unlocked the door and disabled the alarm. All I needed was the key. I got up and stood behind Natalie and began patting her down. Then I reached into the pockets of her shorts with both hands and dug deep. Natalie stirred briefly and managed to get her head about six inches off the table.

"Not tonight, Boris," she said in a slurred Russian accent. "I have headache."

"If you think you've got a headache now, just wait until morning," I said, finally getting my fingers on the key. I slid it out of her pocket, took a quick look at it, then slipped the key into my bag.

I took another look at my watch. Half past two. Time to hit the road. I took a final look at the conga line that continued its meandering journey through the club then walked toward the exit. Outside, I headed straight for the line of taxis waiting to take clubgoers to their destination of choice and hopped into the backseat of the car at the head of the line.

"Where to?" the driver said, glancing at me in the rearview mirror.

"Uh," I said, trying to remember the name of the place. "I'm going to Imperial Motors. It's a used-car lot next to some bar called Evil Ways."

"I know where that is," he said, pulling out into traffic. "You want to go to a used-car lot at this time of night?"

"Yeah, they're having a big sale tomorrow," I said, staring out the window. "I've got my eye on a 2012 Toyota and want to be there when they open."

"Whatever," the driver said, apparently used to chauffeuring strange people around the city.

I laid out my game plan during the ride. It seemed straightforward. Disable the alarm. Find the safe. Grab what was ever inside. Call a cab and make a beeline back to the casino to

242

review what I'd found with Hedaya. I nodded, pleased with my plan.

Piece of cake.

Then I remembered I'd missed dessert.

I did my best to ignore the rumble in my stomach. I glanced out the window and realized we were heading to a section of Vegas I wasn't familiar with. This had to be the dark side of Sin City. Far away from the glitz of the Strip and probably a place where many of the seedier elements lived and preyed. But I was confident that the late hour, now approaching three, would play in my favor. If I was lucky, I'd be in and out of the bar in less than fifteen minutes.

I felt the taxi slow down and then it came to a stop directly in front of the used car lot. I handed the driver a twenty and waved off the change.

"You sure you're going to be okay hanging out here?" he said, glancing at me again through the mirror. "This neighborhood can be pretty sketchy."

"Oh, I have a friend meeting me here," I said, climbing out of the car. "Thanks for the ride."

"Word of advice," he said, putting the car in drive. "If someone comes up to you and asks for your jewelry and wallet, give it to them."

"Got it," I said, closing the back door and waving as he drove off.

I waited until the car disappeared from sight then turned and did my best lumber along the side of the car lot and down a dark alley that led to the back entrance of Evil Ways. When I reached the entrance, I grabbed a small flashlight from my bag and shined it on the keypad. I punched in the six-digit code, MOSCOW, and the door clicked. I pulled it open and stepped inside. I left the door ajar and shined the light around the room that was a combination office-storeroom. Nothing resembling a safe was apparent and I began exploring. I spent about five minutes working my way around the room but came up empty. Then I headed into the bar and glanced around. Deciding that the safe might be hidden somewhere behind the bar, I bent down and shined the light up and down the metal sink and counter but came up empty. But I did see a baseball bat under the counter used, I assumed, to help manage some of the unrulier clientele.

Then I stood up, baffled by my inability to locate the obviously well-hidden repository. I tapped my foot, thought for a moment, then headed back into the office-storeroom. I began peeking behind the stacks of beer and whiskey cases. Then I tried to slide a metal cabinet of drawers away from the wall so I could get a better look. But it wouldn't budge, so I walked to the far side of the room and shined the light on various photographs hanging on the wall. Most of them were shots of Sergei posing with showgirls and minor celebrities. I scowled and shook my head in frustration.

"C'mon Sergei," I whispered as I took another fruitless look around. "Help me out here."

"I doubt if Sergei is going to be able to help. But let me give it a shot."

I slowly wheeled around with an open-mouthed stare.

"Surprise," the voice said without emotion.

"Louie?" I said staring in disbelief at Hedaya's personal chef.

"Hi, Suzy," he said, pointing a pistol at my chest. "I believe you have something I'm looking for."

"Geez, Louie," I said, shaking my head. "I gotta tell you. I did not see this one coming."

"A personal chef," he said with a grin. "Great cover, huh?"

"Yes, it is," I said, nodding. "There's just one thing I don't get."

"What's that?"

"You're not Russian," I said, still stunned.

"No, but I am into money," he said. "Now, if you wouldn't mind handing over that key."

I immediately decided to stall for time.

"What's your hurry?" I said, sitting down. "I've got a whole bunch of questions for you."

"Yes, I'm sure you do," he said, sneaking a peek at his watch. "I suppose I can spare a few minutes before I have to shoot you. Go ahead."

"I guess my first question is why."

"Well, that's a long story," he said, shrugging.

"All the good ones are."

"Indeed," he said, laughing. "Well, my father spent thirty years in the intelligence service. Which one doesn't matter. And I learned two things watching him over the years while I was growing up. The first is that this whole spy versus spy drivel is a total waste of time. All the geopolitical crap about who's going to rule the world is complete nonsense. For all it's worth, you might as well spend your time watching Rocky and Bullwinkle reruns."

"Moose and Squirrel," I said, doing my best Russian accent.

"Exactly. Great show," Louie said, then refocused. "It's really pretty straightforward, Suzy. Empires rise. Empires fall. And people go to war. It's what we do. You know, I doubt if there's been a single time over the past several thousand years when somebody wasn't at war with somebody else. And all the posturing from every side, when you boil it all down, is just a way to justify individuals and countries making a whole lot of money off of other people's misery."

"Interesting take," I said, nodding. I draped a leg over my knee and studied him closely. "So, what's the other thing you learned?"

"That despite the futility of lesson number one, there is a whole bunch of money to be made if you're smart about it."

"Your father taught you that?"

"God, no," he said, laughing. "Mr. Straight Arrow? Not a chance. I learned the second lesson by doing the opposite of what my father would do. If Dad found a nickel on the ground, he'd spend all day trying to find out who it belonged to."

"You're working for the Russians?" I said, still trying to piece it together.

"No, it's nothing like that. Actually, I just started working for Alexi. If you can call it that," he said. "But my days of dealing with that pig are almost over. I just need to get my hands on the key, get whatever is in that safe, and then rework my deal."

"Rework it?"

"Yeah, I don't think I asked for enough," he said, rubbing his chin with the barrel of his gun. "If the information is as damaging as I imagine it is, keeping it quiet has to be worth a whole lot of money."

"I suppose you're right," I said. "Alexi was willing to give me fifty million for it."

"That's a good number," Louie said, sitting down on the edge of the desk and swinging his legs back and forth. "How the heck did you get involved in this thing?"

"Basically, Hedaya asked me to do him a favor."

"Hedaya," Louie said, chuckling and shaking his head. "He does work in mysterious ways."

"It sounds like you're fond of him."

"Are you kidding? I *love* Hedaya. He's a wonderful man and great to work for. But it's time for me to move on."

"And make some real money?"

"Yeah," he said, nodding. "And get away from standing in front of a broiler all day." He frowned. "Brutal."

"Yeah, I get that," I said. "I don't know how Chef Claire does it."

"Ah, Chef Claire," he said, beaming. "One of the most amazing women I've ever met."

"She certainly is," I said.

"For her, being a chef is a calling," Louie said. "To me, it was just something I was good at and could do to pay the bills."

"You've always been attracted to her, haven't you?"

"Of course. What's not to like? I remember the first time I saw her at culinary school. It was like I'd been hit in the head. I literally saw stars. But it was soon clear that we didn't have a future together. When it comes to truly enjoying all that life has to offer, Chef Claire is constrained by her extremely well-defined moral compass."

"Yeah, don't you just hate when that happens," I deadpanned.

"Funny. You know, Suzy. For someone with a gun pointed at her, you're remarkably calm."

"I'm like a duck," I said, doing everything I could to keep him talking.

"Whatever," he said, hopping off the desk. "Now, if you will lead the way back into the bar, I'd like to show you something."

I did as I was told and picked up the pace when I felt him nudge me in the back with the barrel of the gun.

"It's right over there to your left," Louie said.

248

"Where?" I said, peering through the dim light.

"The poster on the wall."

"The one of Al Capone?"

"That's the one," Louie said, coming to a stop. "Sergei was a big fan. All you need to do is reach along both sides of the poster, and you'll feel a couple of clips. Pull them out then slide the poster to one side."

I did as I was told and the poster slid to the right to reveal a safe embedded in the wall.

"How did you know it was here?"

"Sergei had a tendency to get chatty when he drank vodka. Especially when he drank a *lot* of vodka."

"And he told you this was here?"

"Not in so many words," Louie said. "But he did tell me Tuesday night, the day before you guys hit town, that Capone held the secret to success. And all one needed to do was to find the key that unlocked it."

"Pretty easy to figure that one out," I said, shrugging.

"Well, he was drunk at the time," Louie said. "And when I finally figured out what he was talking about, I went straight to Alexi and asked him what it was worth if I could get my hands on whatever is inside that safe."

"Why hasn't he come out here and just broken into the safe?" I said, the question still nagging at me.

"Well, while I told Alexi the name of the place, I also told him that Sergei had mentioned the safe was wired with explosives

249

if anybody tried to break into it. And he agreed to give me a couple of days to find the key."

"That's a pretty good cover story," I said, nodding. "How much did you ask for?"

"Ten million," Louie said.

"But he won't get off that cheap this time, huh?"

"Not if he agreed to give you fifty," he said, waving the gun at me.

"I need to ask you a question," I said, frowning.

"Man, you're relentless. What is it now?"

"You poisoned Sergei's food, didn't you?"

"Yeah, I did," Louie said, giving me a casual shrug. "As soon as he told me about the safe, I figured there wasn't any reason to keep him around."

"You knew he carried the key around with him?"

"I did," he said, nodding. "Sergei happened to mention it."

"Man, he was drunk," I said. "But how were you planning on getting the key from him after you poisoned him?"

"After dinner that night, I was going to give him a tour of the rooftop kitchen," Louie said. "It was something he'd mentioned he wanted to see. After the poison kicked in, I was just going to take the key and then call for help."

"You didn't think people would suspect you?" I said, raising an eyebrow at him.

"Hedaya's personal chef poisoning one of his closest friends?" Louie said, frowning. "Not a chance."

"Not bad," I said, shrugging. "But before you could do that, Kosiny told Sergei he wanted to have a chat with him. And they wandered off to the rainforest."

"Pretty much," Louie said, shaking his head. "But Kosiny screwed that up completely. And when Chef Claire told me about the surgery Josie performed, I knew Hedaya must have had the key."

"Then Alexi told you that someone else had offered to sell it to him and called off your deal, right?"

"Chef Claire was right," he said, nodding. "You are good at this stuff."

"Thanks. So, you figured Hedaya was using Natalie to cut the deal with Alexi."

"As soon as Alexi told me it was a woman who had called him, she was the only one I could think of. That is until I put two and two together when I saw you take the key out of Natalie's pocket."

"What did you put in her drink at the club tonight?"

"Nothing major," he said, shaking his head. "She'll be fine in about an hour."

"Let me guess," I said, grinning at him. "You were going to be the perfect gentleman and escort her home, right?"

"Very good," Louie said, laughing. "Prince Charming to the rescue. I figured I'd be able to get the key from her, get her tucked into bed, and then get out here before the sun came up. But then you decided to stick your nose into it. So, here we are."

251

"Yeah, here we are," I whispered, realizing just how much trouble I was in. "Just one more question."

Louie exhaled loudly and gestured for me to continue.

"Did you throw Kosiny off the balcony?"

"No, that's not my style. And he was a really strong guy," he said. "I'm sure Alexi had someone take care of that. He was furious with Kosiny for screwing things up."

"Olga?"

"Yeah, probably," Louie said. "Okay, Suzy. I'm all talked out. Let's get this over with."

I nodded and took a step toward the safe. I started to reach into my pocket for the key then caught a glimpse of something out of the corner of my eye. I fumbled the key and dropped it, stalling for just a bit more time.

"Klutz," Louie said, shaking his head at me.

"Yeah, sorry about that," I said, kneeling down to pick it up. I grabbed the key then stood up and exhaled loudly.

"Let's go, Suzy," he said. "And I have to say I'm sorry that I'm going to have to shoot you. I really like you."

"Yeah, I can tell," I said, extending the key toward the slot. Then I paused and pulled my arm back. "I was just thinking about something, Louie."

"Now what?" he snapped, his patience exhausted.

"You remember telling me how you saw stars the first time you met Chef Claire?"

"Yeah. What about it?"

252

"Do you believe in déjà vu?"

"What?" he said, frowning at me.

"I think you're about to have one of those moments."

I nodded at something behind him, and he turned his head just in time to get tattooed on the forehead by the bat Chef Claire swung. I heard a loud crack, and Louie dropped the gun then dropped to the floor in a heap.

"Nice shot," I said, grinning at her. "I think that one's going for extra bases."

"Yeah, it was right in my wheelhouse," Chef Claire said, tossing the bat aside and picking up the gun. "But I held back a bit. If I'd swung for the fences, I might have killed him."

"What are you doing here?"

"Saving your butt. What does it look like I'm doing?"

"Yeah, and thanks for doing that. But how did you know I was here?" I said, glancing down at the unconscious chef.

"I saw you leave the club. And when I noticed Louie head out right behind you, I left the conga line and hopped into a taxi and followed him here. What on earth is going on?"

"I'll explain everything when we get back to the suite," I said, reaching for my phone.

"You calling the cops?" Chef Claire said.

"No, there's no need for the cops," I said, waiting for the call to connect. "Hedaya. It's me."

Chapter 29

Ten minutes later, two black SUVs pulled up behind the back of the bar. Hedaya, trailed by three of his security staff, entered and they closed the back door behind them. We waved him into the bar where a very groggy Louie was sitting up and holding a towel against his forehead. Judging by the small pool of blood he was sitting in, Chef Claire had definitely made solid contact.

"Okay," Hedaya said, surveying the scene. "I didn't expect this. You want to catch me up?"

I did.

Hedaya listened closely, and when I finished, he scowled at his personal chef.

"What the hell is wrong with you, Louie?"

"I'm sorry, Hedaya," he said, glancing up with a sheepish look. "You were never even supposed to know about this."

"Do you even know what's in that safe?" Hedaya said.

"No. Nobody does," Louie said. "And that's why everybody was doing everything they could to get their hands on it."

Hedaya thought for several moments then continued.

"How long had Sergei been blackmailing Alexi?"

"Alexi wouldn't say," Louie said. "But based on his recent mood, my guess is a couple of months."

"Did Alexi even know it was Sergei who was putting the squeeze on him?" Hedaya said.

254

"No, not until I told him a couple of days ago."

"Fair enough." He turned to his security guards who were standing nearby waiting for their instructions. "Charlie, put Louie in the back of your SUV. Handcuff his hands and feet and remember to put a blanket down so he doesn't bleed all over the seat. Then the three of you need to clean up this mess. And don't forget to wipe the place down when you're done."

"You got it, Hedaya. What do you want us to do with him?"

"Just put him in the basement with Olga and Maria for now," Hedaya said. "Maybe Olga will do us all a favor and finish him off."

"Will do," Charlie said, nodding at the other guards.

They handcuffed Louie's hands behind his back then helped him to his feet. All three ushered him toward the back door but stopped when Louie protested.

"Just hang on a sec," he said, turning around. "Hey, Chef Claire."

"Yeah?"

"Despite everything, it was great seeing you."

"Yeah, you too, Louie," Chef Claire said, shaking her head.

We waited until they were gone and I handed the key to Hedaya. He inserted it into the slot and opened the door. A thick envelope was sitting inside. Bundles of cash surrounded it. Hedaya grabbed the envelope then turned toward us.

"You guys want some free money?" he said, laughing.

255

"No, thanks," I said, shaking my head. "With my luck, that money is probably from a bank robbery and the serial numbers are on file with the FBI."

"You've been watching too many movies," Hedaya said. "But fair enough. Chef Claire?"

"Absolutely not," she said, shaking her head. "Rule number one. Never take what isn't yours."

"Ah, that pesky, well-defined moral compass," I said, laughing.

"What?" she said.

"Nothing."

"Okay, let's get out of here before the police show up and wonder what we're doing breaking into a dive bar at four in the morning," Hedaya said, tucking the envelope under his arm and closing the safe.

I slid the Capone poster back in place. We followed him outside and climbed into one of the SUVs. I sat in the passenger seat, and Hedaya handed me the envelope then started the car. No one spoke until we reached the Strip. Hedaya took a side street that led to the back of the casino and came to a stop when he got behind a truck making a very early morning delivery.

"They were all still at Shot City when you left?" I said, turning around to look at Chef Claire in the back seat.

"They were," she said.

"They must be passed out in the suite by now, right?"

"I certainly hope so," Chef Claire said. "The last I heard, Jill was challenging your mother to a rematch of their drinking contest."

"Unbelievable," I said. "I wonder if my mom is ever going to act her age."

"Geez, I sure hope not," Chef Claire said. "She squeezes more out of life than anyone I've ever met."

I thought about what she said. Eventually, I nodded.

"Yes, she does, doesn't she?"

Hedaya finally worked his way around the truck and pulled into an underground parking area and came to a stop in one of the spots reserved for him. We climbed out and took a private elevator that opened right outside his office. He held the door for us as we went in then offered us something to drink. Chef Claire and I asked for water.

"What happened to Natalie?" Hedaya said, sitting down with the envelope on his lap.

"Well, at first, I thought she had passed out," I said. "But Louie slipped something into her drink at the club."

"He must have been the one who poisoned Sergei," he said.

"He was," I said, shaking my head sadly.

"You think you know somebody, huh?"

"Louie wanted to get his hands on a lot of money," I said.

"That is not the way to do it," Hedaya said firmly. "Okay, let's take a look at what's inside this envelope."

We both leaned forward in our chairs as Hedaya gently tore the seal. He removed a thick stack of documents and began studying them closely. He carefully read the first page then flipped to the next. After about ten pages, his expression changed from serious to bewildered. Then he started laughing and couldn't stop.

"I don't believe it," he said, flipping back to the first page. "Oh, Sergei. A charlatan to the bitter end."

"What is it?" I said.

"Take a look," Hedaya said, handing me the document.

I stared down at it with Chef Claire peering over my shoulder. After scanning a few pages, I glanced back at her and shook my head in disbelief.

"Recipes?" I whispered.

"Russian recipes," Chef Claire said, frowning.

"He was blackmailing Alexi with a stack of recipes?" I said, staring at Hedaya.

"It certainly looks that way," he said, shaking his head. "Sergei had often talked about getting his hands on a big windfall then leaving and finding a remote spot where nobody knew who he was."

"Take the money and run," I said. "And Alexi completely fell for Sergei's con job."

"Alexi obviously couldn't take the risk about what the information might be," Hedaya said.

258

"I guess when you have a lot of secrets, it doesn't take much to start worrying about what people might have on you," Chef Claire said.

"You'll get no argument from me," Hedaya said, then caught the looks we were giving him. "I mean, yes, that makes a lot of sense."

"What are you going to do with these?" Chef Claire said, flipping through the stack of recipes.

"Nothing," Hedaya said, shaking his head. "Why do you ask?"

"I'm always on the lookout for new recipes," she said.

"Knock yourself out," Hedaya said.

"Oh, goodie," I said, giving Chef Claire a golf clap. "I see a Russian feast in our future."

We glanced at the door when we heard the knock.

"Come in," Hedaya said.

Charlie, the head of security, stepped inside and made eye contact with Hedaya.

"How did everything go, Charlie?"

"It went fine. And we're finished."

"Great. Thank you, Charlie. Well done," Hedaya said.

"Actually, that's not why I stopped by," Charlie said.

"What's wrong?" Hedaya said, frowning.

"We just got a call from one of the guests complaining about the noise coming from 3112."

"Did you say 3112?" I said, glancing at Chef Claire.

259

"Yes," Charlie said.

"Crap."

Chapter 30

With me leading the way, we took the elevator to our floor and as soon as we stepped off the elevator we could hear the pounding bassline coming from down the hall.

"Earth, Wind, and Fire?" I said to Chef Claire as we quickly made our way toward the suite.

"George Clinton," Hedaya said, walking next to us. "I've had him here several times. He puts on a great show."

We came to a stop outside the door. It was no match for the thunderous music coming from the other side. I glanced at Chef Claire, took a deep breath and slid my key card into the slot.

"You ready for this?" I said to her.

"Hey, I watched your mother lick tequila out of a stripper's navel," she said with a shrug. "How much weirder can it get?"

The answer was a lot.

Inside, a couple dozen people I didn't know were dancing. And drinking. A handful of others were getting friendly and really enjoying themselves. I looked around and the first familiar person I spotted was Millie who was sitting on the lap of one of the dancers I recognized from Shot City. He was still wearing his Gladiator ensemble.

"There you are," she said, trying to sit upright and sliding off the dancer's lap onto the floor. "Whoopsie," she said, laughing. "I missed a step."

261

"Who are all these people?" I said, glancing around the suite.

"Just people we met at the club," she said, stifling a burp. "Your mom invited them all back for a party."

Thankfully, the volume of the music lowered. Several people protested, but as soon as they got a look at the size of Charlie, they went straight back to what they'd been doing.

"Where are the dogs?" I said, having a momentary panic attack.

"They're fine," Millie said, waving her hand in the air. "They didn't like the music, so I put them in the other suite. I checked on them a while ago and they're sound asleep."

"Okay," I said, relaxing. "Where's the rest of the gang?"

"Well, let's see," Millie said, looking around. "Josie and Natalie are passed out on the balcony."

"So, Natalie's okay?" I said.

"She's fine," Millie slurred as she waved it off. "She came to while we were still at the club. Then she and Josie started drinking vodka." She swayed back and forth and used an end table to find her balance. "That was a big mistake on Josie's part. I gotta tell you. That Natalie can really put it away."

Hedaya and Charlie looked at each other and laughed.

"Okay," Hedaya said. "I think you've got the situation under control. Let's go, Charlie. Suzy, thanks again. I'll swing by sometime tomorrow before you fly out."

"Sounds great, Hedaya," I said. "And I'm sorry about all the noise."

"This is nothing," he said, shaking his head. "But you might want to try to keep it down the rest of the morning."

"Look at that," I said, glancing out the window at the sun beginning to appear. "It is morning."

We waved goodbye then I looked at Millie who was still trying to focus.

"Where's my mom and Jill?"

"Well, when they got back from the club, they continued their drinking contest," Millie said. "For the record, your mom won."

"Unbelievable," I whispered.

"And the last time I saw Jill she was throwing up in the bathroom," Millie said. "She's probably still in there."

"And my mom?"

"You know, I haven't seen her since the accident."

"What accident?" I said as another wave of panic surged through me.

"Oh, she's fine," Millie said, again waving it off. "She was telling Jill about the time she did track and field in college."

"Your mother ran track?" Chef Claire said.

"Yeah, she did," I said, nodding. "And apparently she was pretty good. But I think she specialized in the field events."

"That's what she said," Millie said, nodding. "Anyway, she was showing Jill how to do the broad jump."

"In here?" I said, stunned.

263

"Yeah. Right over there," she said, pointing at a long stretch of tile that led to a bathroom off the master suite. "That was when the accident happened."

"I'm gonna need a little more, Millie," I said, staring at her.

"More? I think there's still a bunch of tequila left," she said, burping loudly. "Oh, that's better."

"No, I need a little more information. What happened to my mother?"

"Oh, right. Well, she started running, then hopped, landed, and was about to jump when she slipped on the wet tile."

"Oh, my God," I said, fearing the worst. "Where did she land?"

"In the hot tub," Millie said, unable to suppress her smile. "She landed right on her butt."

"But she's okay?"

"She's fine," Millie said, waving it off. "But she sure scared the hell out of the people in the tub."

Chef Claire snorted. I glared at her then refocused on Millie.

"One minute you're relaxing sipping champagne, then some broad jumper splashes down right next to you," Millie said, shaking her head.

"Okay," I said, glancing around. "The party's over."

I turned the music off and put my hands on my hips as I surveyed the crowd who were staring at me.

"Time to wrap it up, folks," I said, pointing at the door. "But the good news is that the breakfast buffet starts in ten minutes."

264

Grumbling and shuffling their feet, people started leaving. Soon, all that was left were a handful of people passed out in various spots around the suite. I glanced at Chef Claire.

"I'll take care of these," I said. "Why you don't make the rounds and make sure we find all of them?"

"Got it," Chef Claire said, heading off to check the bedrooms.

I began waking up the remaining partygoers and soon had them all herded outside. I glanced around then stepped out onto the balcony where Josie and Natalie were sprawled out on lounge chairs and snoring loudly. I walked back inside and slid the glass door shut. Chef Claire came out of one of the bedrooms gently shoving one of the dancers toward the door.

"I found him passed out on a stack of towels in one of the bathrooms," she said, shaking her head as she opened the door. "Have a good day, Billy."

"I doubt if that's going to happen," he managed to mumble on his way out.

Moments later, my mother limped into the living room holding an ice pack on her butt.

"Hi, Mom," I chirped.

"Hello, darling," she said, limping to a couch and sitting down gingerly.

"The broad jump, huh?" I said. "Are you sure you're okay?"

"I'm fine," she said, rubbing her forehead.

"You sure you don't need to go to the emergency room? X-rays? Chiropractor? Maybe a shot of tequila?"

"Please, darling. Just leave me alone," she said, sprawling out on the couch. "Where on earth did you go?"

"Oh, I just went for a little ride," I said, glancing at Chef Claire.

"That's nice," she said, closing her eyes and drifting off to sleep.

I went over, slipped a pillow under her head and placed the ice pack on her bruise. I wrapped a towel around it to hold it in place. I glanced at Chef Claire who was watching me with a grin.

"You're a good daughter," she said.

"Yeah, I have my moments."

Then we both glanced down the hall when we heard the unmistakable sound of someone retching. I grabbed a pillow and a blanket off one of the couches and nodded at Chef Claire.

"C'mon," I said, heading down the hall. "This oughta be good."

We found Jill on her knees with her head over the toilet. Actually, at the moment, it was in it. Her hair was wet and sticky, and I grimaced at the smell. When she realized we were standing behind her, she stared up at us with a look of total despair. Then she dove for the toilet and threw up again.

"Word on the street is that you got into a drinking contest with my mother," I said, doing my best not to laugh.

"Yeah, I lost," she said, wiping her mouth with her sleeve. "Both times."

Chef Claire stepped outside then returned shortly with a wet, warm towel. She began wiping Jill's face and hair then gave it up as a lost cause.

"You ready for a shower?" Chef Claire said. "Or do you need to stay here and throw up some more?"

"I think I better stay here for a while," she said.

"Yeah, that's probably a good idea," Chef Claire said, placing the pillow and blanket on the tile floor. "Try to get some sleep if you can."

"Thanks," Jill whispered.

"Okay, we'll leave you to it," I said, gently placing a hand on her forehead.

"Suzy?" she said, resting her head on the edge of the toilet.

"Yeah?"

"Your mother is an amazing woman."

"You'll get no argument from me."

I turned the light off, and Chef Claire and I headed down the hall to the echoes of another round of retching.

"Chef Claire?"

"Yeah."

"Thanks for saving my life tonight."

"No problem," she said, draping an arm over my shoulder. "Just one suggestion, though."

"What's that?"

"Stop doing stupid stuff."

"Actually, I'm not sure it could officially be called stupid. This one was more of a favor."

"You know what I mean," she said.

"I do," I said, nodding. "I'm sure I'll settle down as soon as Max and I get married."

"You think so, huh?"

"Of course. You know, unless something happens I need to deal with." Then I flinched when she punched me hard on the arm. "Ow. What was that for?"

"You know exactly what it was for," she said.

"You're mean," I said, laughing.

"I'm warning you, Suzy. Don't make me get my bat."

Epilogue

Sunday Redux

After saying our goodbyes to Hedaya and Natalie, who, like Josie, was feeling severely under the weather, we climbed out of the limo he'd kindly provided and headed toward the private jet that would take us back to Clay Bay. Both of them pledged to do everything they could to make the wedding, and just before we boarded, I pulled Hedaya off to the side to have a quiet word with him.

"What did you do with them?" I said, already sweating from the relentless heat.

"I let them go," Hedaya said. "I told them not to come back to the casino in exchange for my not saying a word about what might have happened to Sergei and Kosiny. They seemed satisfied with the offer."

"Did you tell Alexi what you found in the safe?"

"I did not," he said, laughing. "I told him the safe was empty when I opened it."

"You're bad," I said, laughing along. "Did he buy it?"

"Yes, I'm sure he did. I could tell Alexi was already wondering about who might have gotten their hands on it."

"I wish I knew what he is so worried about," I said.

"Me too. It must be good."

"What do you think he's going to do?"

269

"My guess is that he's going to decide he can't take any chances. And when he does, I imagine he'll head straight back to Moscow and try to minimize the damage he thinks is about to land on his head."

"You think Olga and Maria will get reassigned?"

"That would be my guess," he said. "But it's of no concern to me."

"And Louie?"

"Louie was arrested this morning," Hedaya said.

"Really?"

"Yes, Natalie provided an anonymous tip to the Vegas police."

"What's the charge?"

"I'm sure Detectives Williams and Swan will think of something," he said, giving me a mischievous grin. "I just wanted to make a point with Louie. And a murder charge would certainly get his attention."

"I doubt if they'll be able to prove anything," I said, frowning.

"Probably not," he said, shrugging. "As long as he keeps his mouth shut. And I'm certainly not going to testify against him. But as soon as Louie is released, I'm sure he'll be leaving Vegas."

"Because?" I said, staring at him.

"Because I gave him a year's severance and told him to get out of town and not come back."

"That was generous of you," I said.

"When you think about it, Louie wasn't trying to do anything to me," he said. "Like the rest of them, he was simply using my place of business to do it."

"Fair point," I said, nodding. "And your Chinese Democratic Front continues unknown and unabated."

"Yeah, it does, doesn't it?" he said, smiling.

"I really hope you can make the wedding," I said, giving him a hug.

"I think I can. Take care of yourself. And thanks again, Suzy. I will forever be in your debt."

"Pity you can't say the same thing about my mother, right?" I said, laughing. "How much did she end up winning?"

"I don't want to talk about it," he said, waving as he climbed back into the limo.

I climbed the stairs that led to the plane and sat down next to Josie who was wearing sunglasses and had a baseball cap pulled down low over her forehead.

"How are you feeling?"

"Like pond scum," she said, staring straight ahead at the back of the seat in front of her.

"How's your arm?"

"It itches," she said. "But don't worry. The stitches will be out before the wedding. How's your face?"

"Fortunately, it's fading," I said, gently scratching it. Then I sat back and got quiet until the aircraft left the runway and hit altitude. "I can't wait to see the dogs."

271

"Me either," Josie said, glancing over her shoulder at Moose and Squirrel who'd been released from the cages they had to be in until the plane was airborne. "Lucky dogs."

"Yeah, and lucky Millie, too," I said, watching as both spaniels climbed up on her seat, jostling for room to sit.

"I noticed something about those two," Josie said, opening a bag of bite-sized.

"What's that?" I said, grabbing a small handful.

"They're very *present* dogs," she said, still staring straight ahead. "You know what I mean?"

"I think so. But I'm not sure that's the word I would use," I said, nodding. "They've obviously bonded with her already and are definitely sticking very close."

"Well, we're used to that."

"Yeah, we are," I said, glancing back at the dogs who were showering their new best friend with affection. "I think the word I would use is reliable."

"Good word," Josie said, nodding. "Sort of like how you and Max are with each other, right?"

"Yeah, I like that comparison."

"Glad I could help. I'm going to go to sleep now," she said. "Wake me up if we're about to crash."

"Don't start," I said, fighting off my fear of being several miles above the ground going several hundred miles an hour.

Fortunately, the flight was smooth, and we landed ahead of schedule. Max and Sammy met us at the small airfield just outside of town. I hugged and kissed my fiancé until he saw the looks we were getting and began to turn red from embarrassment.

"I missed you too," he said. "But we should probably wait until we get back to the house."

"Good idea," I said, grabbing his hand and leading him toward my SUV.

"What happened to your face?"

"Freezer burn," I said. "Long story."

"I can't wait to hear it," Max said, gently stroking the side of my face.

"Actually, that one barely makes the top ten," I said, shrugging.

"Why is your mother walking like that?" he said, staring at her as she limped her way toward the car.

"Uh, broad jumping accident."

"Just how long is it going to take you to tell me the whole story?" he said, lifting my suitcase into the back of the SUV.

"At least all night," I said, squeezing his hand.

"Works for me," he said, then flinched when he saw the enormous bandage on Josie's arm. "What on earth happened to your arm?"

"I got thirty-seven stitches after being scratched by a thirteen-foot-long Komodo Dragon," she said, slowly climbing into the back seat next to my mother.

"Well, if you don't want to tell me, just say so," Max said, shaking his head.

Josie shrugged and pulled the door closed.

We headed back to the house, and I spent an hour getting reacquainted with Chloe and the rest of the house dogs. Then Josie and I headed down to the Inn to say hello to our other permanent residents. After we were satisfied that everything was in order, we headed back up to the house and ate dinner. Then Max and I went to bed.

Around noon the next day, I was in my office going through some paperwork with Josie when Max poked his head in and told me to turn on the TV. I found the remote and looked at him.

"Try CNN," he said. "You're not going to believe it."

I switched channels and saw an overhead shot of a large body of water. The reporter was recounting the story about how a Russian oligarch's private jet had mysteriously crashed into the Black Sea.

"Do you think that's the same guy you were telling me about last night?" Max said.

"I'd be shocked if it wasn't," I said, staring at the screen in disbelief.

"Man, those guys don't waste any time, do they?" Josie deadpanned. "I guess they weren't very happy to hear that their recipe for Chicken Kiev was on the loose."

I snorted and grinned at her.

"Did they mention any names yet?" I said to Max.

"No, just that the guy was some billionaire who made his money in oil. Apparently, there were two women on the plane with him."

"Wow," I said, still having a hard time believing it. "Maybe I'll give Hedaya a call later and see if he knows any of the details." Then I remembered something my mother had asked me to do. "Is Chef Claire up at the house?"

"No," Max said. "She's already at work."

"My mother wants to go through some final details about the wedding menu."

"Well, she can do it tonight at the restaurant," Max said. "Chef Claire insisted that we eat dinner at C's."

"Why's that?" I said, raising an eyebrow at him.

"She's doing a new special," Max said. "She's got some new recipe she's dying to try out."

"Russian," I said, nodding.

"Yeah, I'm sure I'll be walking fast," Josie deadpanned.

"Really?" I said, making a face at her. "That's the best you got?"

"What can I say?" she said, shrugging. "I'm a bit off my game today. Damn hangover."

I sat back in my chair and replayed the events of the past few days. Despite all the concerns about the mysterious information, and the lengths various people were willing to go to get their hands on it, in the end, five people had lost their lives over a collection of recipes. I shook my head and stared out the window at the dogs who were outside in the play area enjoying the warm summer day.

"What's on your mind?" Max said.

"Oh, I was just sitting here thinking."

"About what?"

"Dinner, primarily," I said, shrugging.

"What about it?"

"Well, after everything that's happened, it better be good."

CPSIA information can be obtained
at www.ICGtesting.com
Printed in the USA
BVHW04s0156091018
529670BV00012B/274/P